Annale[n] ... compati[...] a very u[ncomfortable] marriage. And everyone would see through the sham of it once we were in the spotlight together. The days are long gone when royals marry solely for dynastic reasons."

"Not compatible?"

His voice held a note she couldn't identify, but it made her turn to meet his stare.

Instead of looking argumentative, his expression was even blanker than before. As if he couldn't even be bothered to argue the point. Those brief moments of connection she'd felt earlier must have been in her head.

That bland stare riled her.

Her hands found her hips as she stared into Benedikt's strong features. And noticed again how disturbingly good-looking he was.

Her pulse quickened in self-castigation.

"Exactly. Not compatible. Not attracted."

It was only a partial lie. She might be strangely drawn to him, but he'd given no indication he felt the same way about her. These inconvenient feelings were one-sided. The gleam she'd seen in his remarkable eyes was impatience, not attraction...

Annie West has devoted her life to an intensive study of charismatic heroes who cause the best kind of trouble for their heroines. As a sideline she researches locations for romance whenever she can, from vibrant cities to desert encampments and fairy-tale castles. Annie lives in eastern Australia with her hero husband, between sandy beaches and gorgeous wine country. She finds writing the perfect excuse to postpone housework. To contact her or join her newsletter, visit annie-west.com.

Books by Annie West

Harlequin Presents

The Desert King Meets His Match
Reclaiming His Runaway Cinderella
Reunited by the Greek's Baby
The Housekeeper and the Brooding Billionaire
Nine Months to Save Their Marriage
His Last-Minute Desert Queen
A Pregnancy Bombshell to Bind Them
Signed, Sealed, Married
Unknown Royal Baby
Ring for an Heir

Visit the Author Profile page
at Harlequin.com for more titles.

QUEEN BY ROYAL COMMAND

ANNIE WEST

PRESENTS

ISBN-13: 978-1-335-93991-3

Queen by Royal Command

Copyright © 2025 by Annie West

Recycling programs for this product may not exist in your area.

 Harlequin Enterprises ULC
22 Adelaide St. West, 41st Floor
Toronto, Ontario M5H 4E3, Canada
www.Harlequin.com

Printed in Lithuania

MIX
Paper | Supporting responsible forestry
FSC® C021394

QUEEN BY ROYAL COMMAND

For dear Abby Green

Who organizes the best surprises!

CHAPTER ONE

ANNALENA PAUSED IN the palace's opulent vestibule. All around were the trappings of old wealth and power. The floor of multicoloured marble. Gilded lanterns, huge tapestries and statues by ancient masters.

The triple-height space was topped by a frescoed ceiling that art lovers travelled the world to see. It showed the continents, their people portrayed with improbable romanticism. Grand princes, warriors and scholars. The only women were naked or nearly so, subservient or simpering admiringly. Naked women because that was what the men who'd commissioned it liked to look at, and subservient because that was their place in the world.

Some things apparently hadn't changed in three hundred years.

If Annalena and her grandmother had been male, the powers that be wouldn't have spurned them so insultingly.

'Can I help? Are you here for a tour of the public rooms?'

She turned to see a guide, gesturing to the tourists gathering on one side of the vast space. 'No, thank you. I'm here on business.'

His eyes widened as he tried and failed not to stare at her clothing. As if he couldn't believe she could have business in the royal palace.

Despite her nerves, Annalena felt her lips twitch as he walked away.

She'd thought hard about what to wear to today's meeting. Formal, of course. Initially she'd reached for the suit she'd worn last week to meet the international consortium looking to invest in a joint research project.

But she'd changed her mind and opted for tradition.

Once upon a time she'd hoped the man she'd come to meet was nothing like his father, with his complete disregard for anything except making quick money, no matter the cost to the country. But Benedikt had shown himself to be just as imperious and greedy. Uncaring of tradition and the fact some things were too precious to be destroyed. Her grandmother had raised an eyebrow when she'd seen Annalena ready to travel to the capital. But there'd been laughter in her eyes and approval in her tone when she'd said, 'I see you plan to make a statement, my dear. Good for you. It's a perfect time to remind him we're all custodians of our country. It's not all about his bank balance.'

Annalena made her way across the vestibule towards the royal offices. Her low-heeled shoes tapped purposefully across the expensive marble.

As she neared the closed door, security intervened. 'I'm sorry. This is closed to the public.'

She surveyed the dark-suited man and smiled, belying her thumping heart. For she *was* an interloper, worried at the possibility of failing. Because of her family she'd never had the luxury of being just average, but nor did she belong here. 'I know. I have an appointment.'

She didn't know whether it was a curse or a blessing that so few people in the capital knew her by sight. In the Grand Duchy of Edelforst she was well known. But in Prinzenberg's capital it was different. Her fault for avoiding the place so long.

Who could blame her, given her family history?

Dread pooled in her stomach and a shudder rippled down her spine. She'd grown up viewing this as the sinister centre of the disaster that had engulfed her family.

She'd never set foot in this building and had hoped never to do so. But some things were more important than personal inclination. Besides, she wasn't a child, to be frightened by long ago events.

Yet she couldn't help wondering if Benedikt was as dangerous as his father had been.

The guard looked at her closely. Annalena told herself it was because she didn't look like the usual sort of visitor. She couldn't have betrayed her disquiet. She'd been too well trained to conceal emotions behind a serene mask.

'I wasn't told about a visitor. Who are you seeing?'

Annalena pushed her shoulders back, projecting some of her grandmother's hauteur. 'His Majesty. A ten a.m. meeting.'

'Just a moment, please.'

The guard frowned, half turning away as he spoke into a mouthpiece. Heads turned in their direction.

Good. Let them stare. The more people to witness her arrival, the less chance anyone would dare throw her out.

For the hard-won appointment she'd finally managed to schedule had been cancelled very late last night.

Cancelled without explanation, let alone apology or an offer to reschedule. Given the difficulty she'd had trying to make contact with the man, she shouldn't have been surprised. It was clear she, and her concerns, weren't important enough for royal attention.

That made fury fizz in her veins. She welcomed it as an improvement on nerves.

The people she represented had been patient. They'd followed the proper channels. Yet every attempt to get a hearing had been stymied, every submission met with offensively vague responses.

His Majesty wasn't interested.

He'd soon learn his mistake.

Yet she had to force herself not to press her hand to her stomach where butterflies the size of Alpine eagles swooped and swirled.

The guard turned back. 'I'm sorry, His Majesty's staff have no appointment scheduled.'

'One was made and I've travelled some distance to be here.' She withdrew her phone and showed him the original email.

The man's eyebrows rose as he read her name. He looked decidedly uncomfortable when he met her eyes again. 'I'm very sorry, ma'am, but I was told…' He stood straighter. 'I can't admit you.'

Which was what she'd expected. 'Very well, I'll wait.'

She walked around him to a gilded, antique chair a few metres from the door.

He hurried after her, but not in time to prevent her sitting. 'I really have to ask you to—'

'This is a public area.' She smiled at him. 'Perhaps you'd inform His Majesty's office that I'll wait until it's convenient to see him.'

She knew the King would consider any time inconvenient but she'd given up waiting for him to act decently. If she had to shame him into meeting, so be it.

Faces turned in her direction, the sightseeing group

and staff too. The harried guard whispered urgently into his mouthpiece.

Annalena settled in her seat and tapped her phone. She might as well answer work emails while she waited.

She was absorbed in a report when she heard voices. Without looking up she knew the door to the offices had opened and someone was conferring with the guard.

She checked the time. Half an hour had elapsed. Maybe they'd hoped she'd grow bored and leave. Fat chance!

High heels clacked then stopped before her. Annalena kept reading.

'Excuse me, ma'am.'

It was the guard. She looked up to see he was accompanied by a woman in a sleek charcoal suit, silk shirt and air of sophistication. Her perfect make-up didn't conceal the way her mouth clamped tight.

'Hello,' Annalena said, taking the initiative. 'Are you from his Majesty's office? I—'

'I'm afraid you're wasting your time. The King isn't available.'

Annalena blinked slowly, letting her eyes widen as if no one had ever spoken across her before. Clearly she wasn't going to be offered the courtesy of an introduction either.

The woman lifted her chin. 'You were sent an email. The meeting was cancelled yesterday.'

Annalena let the silence stretch. 'It took well over a month to arrange this meeting and I've come from Edelforst solely to see the King on an urgent matter. I know he's here today so I'll wait and hope space opens up in his schedule.'

The nameless woman frowned, eyes narrowing as she opened her pinched mouth. Annalena forestalled her. 'If you'll excuse me, I'll get back to my work while I wait. His Majesty isn't the only one with a busy schedule.'

She turned to her phone, but not before she saw the woman's jaw clench while the guard beside her veiled a smile.

Annalena's last comment was unnecessary. She'd been raised to be polite, especially given her position. But the woman was rude and Annalena didn't take kindly to bullying. That was what the King of Prinzenberg and his minions tried to do.

So much for her grandmother's insistence the new monarch would be an improvement on the old. Her 'informed sources' had got it wrong.

Heels clicked away and a door closed. Yet it took Annalena a good five minutes to pick up the thread of the report.

She was halfway through it when someone cleared their throat.

It was the burly security guard. Behind him followed a man who deposited a tray on a small table that had appeared beside her. The scent of coffee hit her nostrils and she inhaled appreciatively. Coffee, cream, sugar and cinnamon biscuits.

She beamed at the newcomer, reading his name badge. 'Thank you, Reiner. I didn't have time for morning coffee.' And she'd been too nervous to eat.

He smiled and shook his head, nodding towards the guard before he left. 'It was Udo's idea.'

She turned. 'Udo. That's very kind. I appreciate it.'

Faint colour crept across the big man's cheeks and he murmured something non-committal before returning to his post.

It seemed the King's personal staff were happy to ignore her but other palace employees weren't.

What did that say about the new King of Prinzenberg? That common courtesy didn't matter to him?

Now she found it difficult to concentrate on work. She stared at the screen but it wasn't words she saw. It was Edelforst's wide valleys, the meadows and vast forests, farmland surrounded by towering mountains. The villages and compact towns. The people who loved their land and had struggled hard for generations to support themselves.

Her vision blurred, eyes glazing.

Everything rode on this. She couldn't afford to lose.

'Your Majesty…'

Benedikt shook his head. 'I told you to ditch the title, Matthias, at least when we're alone.' He'd never liked royal pomp. That had been his father's thing.

Thinking about the old man soured his mood. Even now King Karl cast a long shadow.

'Of course.' His private secretary and closest confidant grinned. 'But I worry one day I'll forget in public and call you Benno.' He paused. 'We need to find a gap in your diary.'

Benedikt laughed and leaned back from his desk. 'Good luck. I've seen the timetable for the next month.'

'I'm not talking about later in the month. I mean today. There's a…problem with the schedule.'

Matthias had handled his schedule for years, juggling commitments in Prinzenberg along with Benedikt's business interests across three continents. He couldn't remember problems before. Not in that tone of voice. Not with that frown of disapproval.

'Tell me what happened.'

'Nothing I can't handle, but—'

'Tell me anyway.'

His old friend sighed. 'The same thing. Staff here take it upon themselves to vet who and what you see. They think they're doing right but forget to consult me first.'

'They're still loyal to my father. Or at least his ways.'

Benedikt's mouth tightened. He'd been young when he discovered how little he liked his father's ways. Which was why, from the time he'd had any say in it, he'd spent so much time outside Prinzenberg even though he loved it. He'd only returned full-time following his father's recent death.

'They'll learn. I'll make sure of it. But it takes time.' Matthias sighed. 'Meanwhile, you have a visitor.'

'If he's not on the schedule I haven't got time.'

'She *was* on the schedule. I put her there. But someone decided she didn't need to see you.' He let that sink in. 'She turned up anyway. She's been in the palace vestibule for almost three hours. I've only just found out.'

'Three hours! In the vestibule?' He paused, watching Matthias's expression turn ever more sombre. It seemed worse was to come. 'Who is she?'

'The Grand Duchess of Edelforst's granddaughter. Princess Annalena.'

What was a member of Edelforst's most senior family doing here? What administrator in their right mind thought it okay to put her off and not tell him?

As if Benedikt didn't have enough to deal with. His coronation was fast approaching and he was still fighting spot fires left by his father, made more difficult by the fact his father had been secretive about so much. Karl had jealously guarded his business dealings as well as his power and prestige, even from his heir.

Relations between the Grand Duchess and Benedikt's father had been frosty, if not downright inimical. As the Grand Duchy was a semi-autonomous province of Prinzenberg, in the end his father had left the place to run itself.

The Grand Duchess had a lot of power in the province, which had traditionally been ruled along matriarchal lines. Outside her province she technically had no political authority but she was respected, even revered nationally, though she hadn't been seen outside Edelforst for years.

Insulting her granddaughter was *not* how Benedikt wanted to begin their relationship. He'd planned to visit but kept being delayed as he uncovered yet more urgent problems left by his father.

There was a knock on the door before it opened. He sighed and rose, an apology forming for her wait. But surprise caught his tongue as Matthias ushered her in.

The young woman's dark blonde hair was plaited, arching over her head in an old-fashioned coronet that added to her height. Instead of modern dress she wore a dirndl of forest green, figured with silver. A decorative apron of pale green covered her skirt, the fabric betraying its cost with a shimmer of silk.

Her tightly fitted, laced-up bodice moulded a narrow waist and round breasts, the low décolletage revealing the edge of an embroidered white blouse beneath it.

There was no cleavage on show and her skirt fell just below her knees but Benedikt's skin prickled in instant male awareness.

His skimming glance rose to the dark green velvet ribbon around her throat with its silver pendant. Worn like a choker, it emphasised her slender neck and the soft-looking skin sloping down to her breasts.

Benedikt swallowed, shocked by his instant response. His fingers twitched and his lower body hardened, his breath stalling.

The dirndl was the national dress of Prinzenberg, rarely worn in the capital except at festivals. Even in her province of Edelforst, it wasn't worn daily. His parents had regarded it as terminally old-fashioned and he'd thought of it as appealing but country cute.

This woman wore it like a weapon.

She looked magnificent. And incredibly sexy.

His first appraisal took in her traditional clothes and slender body. His second lingered on her face. Taking in eyes the green of a mountain tarn and lips that curved like the proverbial Cupid's bow.

Dimly Benedikt was aware of his heartbeat quickening and her eyes widening as she stared too, looking almost as taken aback as he was.

His vision flickered as something hard and fierce pulsed between them. Something he felt low in his belly and high in his tightening chest.

Imagination, he told himself. The result of too little sleep and too many hours unravelling the murky web of his father's business dealings.

Matthias broke the silence, murmuring introductions before bowing his way out. Leaving them alone.

Benedikt moved from behind his desk. 'It's a pleasure to meet you, Princess.'

He held out his hand just as she lowered her gaze and bobbed in a brief curtsey that was graceful but not at all subservient.

His hand fell. She mustn't have seen him reach to shake her hand.

When she lifted her head her steady stare set off warning bells. She didn't look like a supplicant. Nor a well-wisher. Her even features were composed, almost expressionless. Too expressionless.

'My sincere apologies that you had to wait to see me. That was most unfortunate.'

'As you say. But I managed to get some work done while waiting.'

Her words were even yet held a note of provocation. A reminder that her time was valuable too?

He gestured for her to precede him to a pair of leather lounges facing each other. 'Please, take a seat.'

There was a refined rustle of silk as she passed him and he found himself watching her graceful walk. Not the hip-swinging sway of a woman in high heels to which he'd grown accustomed. Her movements were more fluid and she sank onto the chesterfield with a grace that made him imagine her swirling around the palace's grand ballroom in a long gown.

'I only learned a few minutes ago that you were here.'

Her eyes widened before her forehead crinkled in a frown. 'Yet I spoke to one of your staff soon after I arrived.'

She doesn't believe a word you said.

It was there in her carefully bland expression and too tight jaw. And the angle of her chin, not precisely aggressive but not compliant either.

Benedikt wondered what it would be like to have this woman compliant, or, better yet, pleased and eager to see him. His palms prickled with a phantom sensation as he imagined holding her. Her chin would lift, not in pride or wariness, but to bring her lips closer to his.

Adrenaline shot through his bloodstream, making his pulse pound.

He took a seat opposite and banished the fantasy. Later, when there was time, he'd unpick how she'd planted such thoughts in his hitherto pragmatic brain.

Unlike his father, he *never* let sex interfere with his obligations.

'My private secretary will get to the bottom of the miscommunication. In the meantime, again, my apologies. Can I offer you refreshments?'

'Thank you, no. I had some recently.'

No breaking bread with the enemy, then.

She certainly wasn't here as a friend, come to congratulate him on his accession to the throne.

His father had complained about her feisty grandmother, getting in the way of his modernisation plans.

When he was younger Benedikt hadn't paid much attention other than to silently applaud anyone courageous enough to get in his father's way. It seemed the old lady's granddaughter had the same strength of character.

'If you don't mind,' she said, sitting straighter, 'I'll get straight to business.'

'By all means. Which business, specifically?'

Which business?

Annalena sucked in an indignant breath. As if he didn't know full well! There could only be one reason.

How dared he pretend not to know?

He even softened his question with a slight smile as if he really cared.

As if she could be swayed from her purpose by that!

Annalena chose not to think about that moment of shocked reaction when she'd entered the room and seen him in person for the first time. Tall, well-built and suave in his expensive suit, he'd made her pause as an unfamiliar sensation triggered inside her.

His features were arresting, bold and attractive, enhanced by an intriguing groove down one cheek when he smiled. That, and the laughter lines at his eyes, gave an impression of warmth. As did those golden-brown eyes that contrasted so appealingly with his dark hair. But she wasn't fooled. He was as hard and autocratic as his father. They even had the same stubborn, angular jaw.

'The dam, of course.'

'Ah.' He paused, his expression impassive. 'What aspect did you want to discuss?'

Annalena resisted the urge to grind her teeth. He might have been asking what cake she'd like with her coffee.

Did he really think so lightly of their concerns?

You know the answer to that. He doesn't care any more than his father did. That's why you're here. Just because he looks...appealing doesn't mean he's even halfway decent.

She pinned on a cool smile, thankful that his arrogance temporarily banished her worry and her ingrained fear at being in the palace where King Karl, the bogeyman of her childhood, had lived. 'All of it. You know the whole idea is disastrous. I've come to make sure it's stopped.'

Now she got a reaction. His eyes no longer looked complacent. They widened in shock. His dark, angular eyebrows jerked down above his nose and his mouth lost its easy half-smile.

Obviously he didn't like head-on confrontation.

In which case he should have done something about this much earlier. For a moment satisfaction flared, but she stifled it. This wasn't about her but about keeping Edelforst safe.

He smoothed out his frown and spread his hands in an apparently open gesture. 'I'm happy to take you through whatever aspect of the project concerns you. But as for stopping it... That's impossible. It's a tremendous opportunity for the country and will bring huge benefits long term.'

Annalena curled her hands over the arms of her chair. 'Of course it's possible to stop it. Work hasn't begun.'

He shook his head, his lips curving in a half-smile, as if humouring her. But there was no smile in his eyes. 'It's not that simple. You may not be familiar with the ins and outs of commercial projects but commitments have been made. Contracts are in the final stages of negotiation.'

Patronising man! She might not have managed a hydro-electric project, but she knew about commercial negotiations, both on her grandmother's behalf and in her own work. Botanical research that identified compounds with potential medical and other uses was highly prized.

'If contracts are being negotiated they haven't been signed.'

'But statements of intent have, with penalty clauses if the project doesn't proceed.'

'You were so sure you could force this through, despite the opposition?'

'Opposition? You've been misled. A thorough feasibility study was undertaken and no negative issues were found that outweighed the benefits of the scheme.' He smiled, a charming smile that Annalena guessed would make a lot of women melt. Even she felt a tickle of appreciation low in her body. 'I'm happy to explain the scheme and put your mind to rest.'

Put her mind to rest!

How dared he? He made her sound as if she were too ignorant to understand what the scheme involved. As if she'd come here on a whim. She'd guarantee she knew more about it than he did.

Now she knew how he worked. He used charm to cloak his ruthlessness instead of the aggressive bluster his father had employed. One had threatened people into compliance and this one showed friendly concern that was barely skin deep.

Contempt fired in her blood.

He intended to brush their concerns aside. To downplay them and carry on regardless. Because, like his father, he had the power.

Her heart thudded so hard and fast she almost put a hand to her breast to calm it. Instead she kept her hands where they were, a lifetime's lessons in control and decorum coming to her aid.

She drew a slow breath. She'd come hoping they'd discuss this sensibly and he'd see reason. She'd hoped he wasn't like his father.

Above all, she'd hoped he wouldn't force her hand.

Instead he was fobbing her off.

'There's nothing I could say to dissuade you?'

His smile was sympathetic. Or was that pitying? 'I'm afraid not. But—'

'Please! No more weasel words about tremendous opportunities and the public good. We both know they're false.'

She'd shocked him. He looked almost comically stunned, as if no one ever called him on his lies. If the situation weren't so dire she might find it amusing.

But this wasn't funny. They'd done everything they could. Submitted detailed reports and evidence. Experts had talked at length with royal administrators. From the moment the massive dam was mooted under his father's reign, everyone from her grandmother to scientists, sociologists and farmers in Edelforst had pleaded to save a huge proportion of their land from being flooded.

No one had listened.

There was only one way to stop this disaster, but it meant doing something so drastic Annalena had desperately hoped to avoid it. The thought of inserting herself further into this awful place filled her with dread. But this wasn't about her.

Shoring up her resolve, she drew some papers from her pocket and held them out, pleased her fingers didn't tremble. Though from this moment, her life would never be the same.

Benedikt of Prinzenberg rose and took the papers. 'What are these?'

'The documents that will ensure the dam isn't built.' Annalena sucked air into constricting lungs. 'Proof you're not the legitimate ruler of Prinzenberg. I am.'

CHAPTER TWO

SHOCK RAN THROUGH Benedikt like an electric current through copper wire. His fingers twitched and he had to firm his hold on the papers.

She was serious! Or the best actor he'd ever seen. He read hints of unease despite her raised chin and imperious stare. But she didn't back down.

For a stunning moment he felt a searing lightness, a dazzle of relief.

Because he hadn't wanted to be King. Monarchy meant King Karl and he'd never wanted to be like his father.

He'd seen hints of his father's darkness in his own soul long ago and feared following in his footsteps. The impatient, remorseless part of him that triumphed in getting his own way. In winning no matter the odds stacked against him. The pride. The thrill he got from risk-taking that in the past had verged on recklessness.

But he loved his country. He'd reconciled himself to his duty, knowing Prinzenberg needed him, now more than ever. With his father's death, he'd shouldered his inherited burdens, despite his old fear that royal power might exacerbate those ruthless tendencies he'd tried to conquer.

'You're accusing me of being a usurper?'

She drew a deep breath. Benedikt fought not to notice

her breasts rise against her constraining bodice. A tactic to distract him?

'You're not entitled to be King. The coronation you're planning in a couple of weeks is a farce.'

Her words were as good as a slap to the face. Benedikt felt a muscle spasm in his jaw.

Did she really think she could get away with such a ridiculous lie?

He looked at the documents in his hand. The first was a copy of a marriage certificate, the writing old-fashioned but clear. It recorded the wedding thirty years ago between Alexandra Cecile Adelgunde Luise Von Edelforst to Christian Maximilian Eitel Luitpold Von Prinzenberg.

Benedikt's breath escaped silently, leaving his lungs empty.

Christian of Prinzenberg.

Once the Crown Prince. So much loved by the people that his name still was spoken with reverence, something that had always annoyed Benedikt's father.

All the country knew Christian had died tragically young and unmarried.

Benedikt sank onto the lounge, head spinning.

He read the certificate again, frowning. It had to be a forgery. He flipped the page over and found a copy of another certificate, this time a record of birth. For Annalena Alexandra Christiane Luise Von Prinzenberg, dated eight months after the wedding.

Von Prinzenberg.

It was the royal name, held only by the country's ruler and their direct family.

Despite knowing this had to be fraudulent, Benedikt felt a tickle of unease track down his spine.

After Christian then his father the King died in quick

succession, Benedikt's father, Karl, had inherited the title. He was a distant cousin of Christian's. It had taken almost a year of careful checking and deliberation before he was officially named heir to the throne, his name changing to Von Prinzenberg. The name Benedikt now carried.

He lifted his gaze to the woman opposite. She sat straight-backed, knees bent and ankles crossed neatly. Hands clasped in her lap. Only the rapid and rise and fall of her breasts and the pulse thrumming at the base of her neck betrayed she was anything other than completely composed.

'You expect me to fall for this fraud?'

She flinched minutely but held his stare with those deep green eyes. 'It's not a fraud. It's the truth.'

Benedikt shook his head. 'These papers don't prove anything.'

'On the contrary.' She leaned forward. 'They prove I'm the rightful ruler. I'm the only child of Prince Christian, who should have been King after his father. I'm his rightful heir, born before your father took the crown.'

'If you believe this fabrication.' Benedikt's hand fisted, crumpling the papers.

'You think by destroying those, you can hide the truth? You believe *me* so naive as to bring the originals?' She sat back, eyebrows lifting. 'Those are copies. The originals are held safe. Don't think you can bury the truth.'

'I'm not in the habit of burying anything.'

Her huff of disbelief was loud in the thick silence. 'Like father, like son,' she murmured.

Benedikt opened his mouth to challenge her but stopped. He more than most knew his father had kept secrets, some shameful. But he couldn't let himself be distracted.

'How do I even know you're Annalena, granddaughter of the Grand Duchess of Edelforst?'

She looked the right age and he knew the real Annalena was blonde. He'd seen her once as a child on a rare visit to the province.

That had to be it. She was some crazy impostor. But why pursue a lie that would be easily found out?

'You can call my grandmother, and there are people here in the capital who can vouch for me. Meanwhile…'

She dug out a small card and passed it to him. It was a driver's licence, worn around the edges. It looked real. The only anomaly was that the woman in the photo wore a plain white T-shirt and her hair in a high ponytail.

He stared. It was the same woman but the difference from the one sitting here was enormous. The picture showed someone relaxed and half smiling, with none of the buttoned-up tension emanating from the figure before him.

He put the licence and papers on the seat beside him. They'd be investigated fully.

'It's still not true. You can't be Queen.'

One eyebrow rose mockingly. 'You should know Prinzenberg was one of the first European countries to acknowledge the rights of female heirs. Males don't take precedence when it comes to inheriting the throne.'

He stopped her with a slicing gesture. 'I'm fully aware of our constitutional history. It was an essential part of my education *as son of the King.*'

Her lips curled in a grimace, the first evidence of unfettered emotion he'd seen in her. Her tone was heavy with repugnance. 'He might have ruled but that doesn't mean he had the right to.'

Deep inside, Benedikt felt the truth of that. Not because he had doubts about his father's right to inherit the throne, but because the country had deserved someone far better. Someone who cared more for it than themselves.

He breathed out slowly. That was his mission, and his obligation, to redress his father's wrongs and be the head of state his country needed. He hoped he was up to it, that his father's taint didn't undermine him.

'Of course he had the right. He was the previous King's closest surviving relative.'

She merely shook her head as if the nonsense on the papers she'd brought were true.

He'd never been gullible, even as a child. Growing up with a father like his had ensured that. Karl had been cold, emotionally abusive and regularly twisted the truth to suit himself.

Benedikt rubbed the back of his neck where tension clamped. The six weeks since his father's death had been taxing. His schedule was diabolical and he couldn't waste more time on this.

'I'm not interested in fairy tales. I *know* this can't be true.'

In the afternoon sunlight her braid gleamed like gold as she tilted her head. Far from looking put out, she appeared curious. As if he were an intriguing specimen to be examined. 'How can you be certain?'

'Because if your story were true, your mother would have told the old King she was pregnant with his grandchild and secured your place on the throne.'

His guest didn't look flustered. 'He didn't outlive my father for long. The King was already dying when my father was killed in that accident.'

Impatience made Benedikt grit his teeth. 'That doesn't explain why she didn't come forward. Why hide you? Why keep the supposed wedding secret?' He rose. He'd had enough. 'Your story doesn't hold water. I don't know what your game is but you didn't think it through.'

He grabbed the papers, about to turn away.

'They kept the wedding secret because the old King was pressuring my father into an arranged marriage. He was gravely ill and wanted his son married before he died. He'd chosen someone but Christian, my father, couldn't marry her because he was in love with my mother.'

'Fairy tales,' Benedikt repeated. 'That's all you offer me.'

'It's true!'

She shot to her feet, eyes ablaze, and Benedikt found himself snared by the emotion he read there. It punctured his estimate of her as coolly conniving. She looked full of passion.

His pulse kicked.

'The King was worried about the country's finances and wanted him to marry the daughter of an American billionaire. Someone with plenty of money to invest in Prinzenberg.'

A sliver of ice punctured Benedikt's chest.

Someone like his mother.

Karl had been charming when he chose and Benedikt's mother had fallen for his wooing, then lived to regret her choice, finally realising he cared more for her money than her. Karl's pretence of affection had ended after several miscarriages and the stillbirth of a second son. With the news she'd never be able to give him a spare heir.

Benedikt's most vivid childhood memories were of her distress at her husband's casual cruelty. If he had a choice he'd never marry. For him the very idea was weighted with pain and negativity, with trauma. Fury rose that this stranger should involve his mother, a woman who'd endured so much, in this scam. Benedikt still felt her loss deeply, and his grandfather's.

He stalked across, straight into Annalena's space. If that was who she really was. 'I've had enough of your games.'

He'd long ago learned to curb the volatile anger that could provoke reactions he'd later regret. But he had his limits.

Serious eyes met his with no trace of fear. 'My parents were in love but my father didn't want to disappoint *his* father so he stalled for time. Then they discovered I was on the way. They married in Edelforst with my grandmother's blessing. My father left, intending to choose the right time to announce their marriage, but he made my mother promise *not* to come to the capital. He insisted she keep their marriage and her pregnancy secret until he took her there.'

Despite himself, Benedikt was intrigued. It had the elements of a good yarn if nothing else.

'That doesn't explain why she didn't come forward later. Why no one else heard about this supposed marriage.'

Annalena crossed her arms, not pugnaciously but, he realised, defensively. Her shoulders curved in. Suddenly she looked vulnerable, making him notice for the first time how much smaller she was than he. Her feisty attitude had eclipsed so much.

'She was protecting me. She died soon after I was born and my grandmother stayed quiet for the same reason.'

'And you needed protection from…?'

'I was only a few weeks old when your father was proclaimed heir to the throne.'

'Still time to assert your claim. Why didn't they?'

She straightened, arms unfolding and shoulders pushing back. She tilted her jaw and, despite the fact she only came up to his shoulder, managed to look down her nose at him. As if she really were Queen and he some ragtag imposter.

'Because of what my father said before he left that last time. He wasn't looking forward to telling his father he'd married for love not duty. He didn't want to disappoint his sick father. But he had something else on his mind. A series of accidents had dogged him in the capital. Potentially fatal accidents.'

'You're saying he thought someone was trying to kill him?'

'Someone else was vying for power. Someone who saw the old King's illness as an opportunity. My father didn't want to reveal he was married until he had concrete proof and had neutralised the danger.'

She went on before he could interject. 'My father left Edelforst on a Sunday night and by Wednesday morning he was dead. In a car accident on a road he knew like the back of his hand. The first report mentioned an oil spill on the road at the only spot where the side plunged into a ravine. But the official, final report made no mention of it. There were other anomalies—'

'You forget there was no one else in line to inherit the throne. No one *vying* for power.'

Her expression changed, defiance and sadness replaced with something like regret. 'No one except the orphan who'd been raised at the palace beside the Crown Prince as an act of charity. Someone ambitious and older than Christian, who chafed at the fact he could never rise to the same heights of power. Someone who, within weeks of the Crown Prince's death, quietly married the American heiress whom the old King had favoured.'

Benedikt's blood froze, his skin turning clammy with horror.

'Your father. Who later became King Karl.' Her voice was implacable, her words missiles. 'That's why my family kept the marriage and my parentage secret. They didn't want him to kill me too.'

CHAPTER THREE

'WE HAVEN'T BEEN able to disprove it, but we've only had a couple of hours.' Matthias was grim as he met Benedikt's gaze across the desk. 'The priest who supposedly officiated at the wedding *was* the priest at that church on that date. He's retired but still lives nearby. The other witnesses, including the Grand Duchess, still live in Edelforst.'

'And?' There had to be more.

'I spoke to the priest. A trusted staff member is heading there in person to conduct an interview, but I knew you'd want an initial report.'

Benedikt nodded, appreciating his assistant's thoroughness but wishing he'd get to the point.

'You're not going to like this. The old man said he remembered the ceremony perfectly. He said it was the honour of a lifetime to marry the Crown Prince to the Princess he'd baptised in the very same church.'

Benedikt fell back in his seat, the air expelling forcibly from his lungs.

Was there no end to this nightmare?

He'd known Annalena of Edelforst was trouble from the moment she marched into this room and the floor shifted beneath his feet.

He'd put that visceral response down to tiredness from

overwork. Taking over the labyrinthine mechanics of his father's commercial empire and trying to separate it from royal responsibilities and assets was even harder than he'd anticipated. His father had melded the two, running private business interests and the country to benefit himself and his cronies. Even his staff ran the country like a private fiefdom.

Then in strides Princess Annalena, who it seemed really was who she claimed, accusing him of being a usurper.

And his father of murder.

Benedikt had detested his father. The man had all but destroyed Benedikt's mother and set an example to his son of the sort of man he *didn't* want to become.

But murder? Even Karl wouldn't stoop to that.

Yet Benedikt felt a niggle of unease.

King Karl had been inflexible, selfish and devious despite his outward charm. Every stone Benedikt turned over, stepping into his shoes, revealed something questionable if not downright corrupt.

Grabbing the arms of his chair, he scooted forward, leaning across the desk. 'Did the priest give a reason for keeping the wedding secret?'

'The Prince and the bride's mother, the Grand Duchess, swore him to secrecy. He only talked now because the Grand Duchess said that after all this time, if he were asked he should tell the truth.'

'The truth!' Benedikt shot to his feet, shoving his chair back and stalking away. 'It's all a lie.'

'I did manage to track down the other witnesses.'

Benedikt spun around, but from Matthias's expression he knew that wasn't good news.

'Apart from the Grand Duchess, there were two. One was and still is her lady-in-waiting. I haven't spoken to either of them. I thought that was better done in person.'

Benedikt nodded. If the old lady was part of this scheme they'd have to tread carefully. As for her lady-in-waiting, she'd do whatever her mistress ordered. Who even had ladies-in-waiting any more?

'And the other witness? His name seemed familiar.'

'I spoke to him by phone. He had the same story as the priest. Brought in to witness a wedding but asked not to reveal the details until now.'

'How did he sound? Plausible?'

Matthias pinched the bridge of his nose before meeting Benedikt's gaze. 'Very. He was a lawyer then. He's now a judge with a reputation for probity and fairness. His name was familiar because he's on our list to help manage your programme of law reform.'

A harsh laugh escaped Benedikt. 'The old lady really pulled out all the stops with this plot, didn't she?'

'If it's a lie, it's a very good one. But we've only just started investigating. Face-to-face interviews might yield different results. Plus we have to examine the original documents.'

'I want someone to dig out all available information on Prince Christian's car smash.' Benedikt paused, hating the hollow feeling in the pit of his stomach. 'Do we have my father's diaries for the period?'

Like his predecessors, King Karl had kept a daily diary of royal business.

'No. Apparently your father only began the practice after he was crowned. And, instead of writing it himself, he had his secretary note down key business.'

So there'd be no confessions about crimes he might have committed. Benedikt didn't know whether to be pleased or disappointed.

'Thanks, Matthias.' Benedikt leaned one hip against the desk. 'Keep me informed of progress.'

This couldn't have come at a worse time, in the lead up to his coronation. Maybe that was why they'd chosen it.

'Have you decided what you're going to do?'

Benedikt met his sympathetic stare. 'What can I do except find out what really happened?'

Unlike his father, he didn't brush aside inconvenient truths. If her story were true...

It didn't bear thinking about.

Prinzenberg was in a worse state than he'd thought, public monies siphoned off to private individuals and a whiff of corruption where there was big money to be made. Benedikt had worked hard to prepare himself to become King one day but it would take all his skills, knowledge and time to set his country on the right track again.

The idea that a woman who'd never been near the royal court, much less the machinery of government, could take his place...it made his blood run cold.

Prinzenberg couldn't afford an amateur. It needed strong, strategic government. Benedikt was far from perfect but he was a highly successful businessman, thanks to his grandfather's mentoring, and he'd been raised to understand politics, public service and foreign diplomacy.

Matthias inclined his head in the direction of the room where Annalena awaited his return. 'And the Princess?'

Benedikt rolled tight shoulders. 'Let me worry about her.' He opened a desk drawer, reaching for headache tablets. 'Believe me, you've got the easier job.'

'Frankly, my dear, I'd never realised the practical implications of your career. It's fascinating, the work you're doing.'

Colonel Ditmar smiled warmly before taking a bite of

cherry pastry. As a child she'd known him well, the kindly man with an engaging twinkle who always had time for a rather lonely little girl.

She hadn't seen him for years, though he still visited her grandmother. Seeing him reminded her how time marched on. He had the same upright bearing, bushy moustache and gravelly voice, but his moustache and hair were white now, and his face, like her grandmother's, was lined by age.

Annalena had been raised by a generation older than the parents she'd never known. It struck her how precious her time with those dear people was.

She shoved aside the thought of a world without her amazing Oma, instead recounting for the colonel an amusing story about a field trip fraught with complications.

His laughter eased the tension knotting her shoulder blades. It almost made her forget they shared coffee and cake not in her grandmother's elegant sitting room, but in an ostentatious salon full of ornate gilding and uncomfortable chairs.

Was there *any* room in the sprawling palace designed for comfort rather than show? She felt the constraining shadow of King Karl and his son in the very walls.

As if on cue, a door in the white and gilt panelling swung open and a tall figure appeared. Wide shoulders filled the space, then in stepped the man who called himself King.

Easier to think of him in those terms than as Benedikt. That was too dangerously informal. Annalena didn't have his measure. She didn't believe he'd resort to violence like his father but she didn't trust him. She couldn't let down her guard. Not when in one short interview he'd completely upset her equilibrium.

Upset it? The first time their eyes met it felt like an earthquake resonating from the pit of her stomach, overwhelming her body in waves of… What? Yearning? Recognition?

She roped in dismay. It would take a remarkable man to make Annalena yearn at first sight.

Her parents had fallen for each other at first sight. Far from finding that sweet or inspirational, for Annalena that had been a cautionary tale. Their love had been doomed, leaving her mother a widow while still a bride. Then she'd died of a broken heart as much as from illness, leaving her daughter orphaned. No wonder Annalena had never dreamt of romance. As for being swept off her feet…!

No, Benedikt might be remarkable but, she told herself, for all the wrong reasons.

Yet as he crossed the room, a warm smile easing his features as he greeted the colonel, Annalena felt *something*. A fluttering in her chest. The suspicion of an ache that for a moment left her breathless.

She watched him shake the old man's hand, refusing to let him rise from his seat, though protocol demanded it. Or would if he really were King.

Annalena swallowed convulsively as unease raised goosebumps across her skin. She'd done the right thing, revealing the secret of her birth. Every other avenue they'd tried had failed. But had she unleashed something larger than she'd imagined?

He turned, eyes appraising, and suspicion solidified into an atavistic fear that she'd set in motion something she couldn't control.

'Princess Annalena, I hope you've enjoyed your afternoon tea.'

She inclined her head, refusing to use the title he claimed. 'Thank you, yes. The colonel and I are old friends. It's been wonderful to catch up. Such a coincidence we should be visiting the palace at the same time.'

And such a convenient way for you to check I really am who I say. The colonel wouldn't be fooled by an imposter.

One dark eyebrow rose and she had the unnerving sense her opponent read her mind.

She almost wished he could. He had such a confident air it would do him good to realise it took more than good looks to impress a thinking woman.

His eyes narrowed on her then flared wide, more gold than brown. Heat bloomed inside her and she hurriedly turned to her companion. She was *not* discomfited. She was simply remembering her manners.

'Colonel—'

'It's been so good to see you, dear Annalena. But I must get on. Business to see to, you know.'

He rose and she stood too. 'Of course. It's been lovely. I'll pass on your regards to my grandmother.'

He leaned in and kissed her cheeks, the brush of his moustache and the scent of butterscotch taking her straight back to childhood.

Then he was gone, leaving her with the brooding man who ruled this place.

Suddenly she felt very alone.

Annalena straightened her spine after picking an imaginary piece of fluff off her skirt. 'Are you at least convinced now that I am who I say?'

'There seems little doubt.' He moved nearer, not as close as the colonel had been, yet she *felt* his presence as a physical weight pushing against her. She couldn't quite get her breath, her breasts straining against fabric that suddenly felt too tight. He extended his arm and it took all her self-control not to flinch. 'Your driver's licence.'

'Thank you.' She took it, careful not to brush his fingers. 'I assume you had it checked.'

'Naturally. Proving your identity is the first necessary step.' He gestured to her seat. 'Won't you sit?'

Annalena subsided onto the chair and watched him take the colonel's seat. He looked completely composed and in control. She didn't know what she'd anticipated but was annoyed at his equanimity. Especially since she felt anything but calm. 'And the next step?'

He reached for a poppy-seed pastry, taking a large bite and chewing before answering. 'Sorry, I didn't have time for lunch.'

She folded her arms. 'I know the feeling.'

His huff of laughter surprised her, sending a skittering sensation through her middle. His sombre eyes crinkled at the corners making him look…

Deliberately she turned towards the generous spread she'd been too keyed up to enjoy. A slice of chocolate gateau caught her eye. If ever there was a day for chocolate this was it. She helped herself, a welcome distraction from this man who so confused her.

She didn't trust him, yet being with him made her feel energised and self-aware. The sharpness of her breathing. The cinch of fabric at her waist. The weight of her mother's locket at her throat. The scrape of her nipples against her bra.

'The next step?' she asked as she slid a fork through dense chocolate and fluffy cake.

'Proving your claim to the throne is false, of course.'

His absolute certainty surprised a laugh out of her. All the proof she'd given him and she hadn't even created doubt in his mind. 'Good luck with that.'

'You find this amusing? You're enjoying yourself?'

Now she heard it, not uncertainty but steely threat. He wasn't as sanguine as he appeared.

Her grandmother had spoken in scathing terms about his father. Was the man before her just as callous? As ruthless? It was a chilling possibility. But nothing would happen to her under his roof. Too many people knew she was here.

Seeking distraction, Annalena popped a piece of cake into her mouth, focusing on the rich flavour and texture, rather than the scorching glare turned her way. She swallowed and licked her bottom lip.

'If you think this is how I get my kicks you really are out of touch. No person in their right mind would do what I've done today for fun. I didn't *want* to come. I didn't *want* to reveal the truth about my parents. I'm happy with my life, thank you very much, and I'd rather get on with it.' She put down the delicious but barely touched cake, the fork rattling on the plate. 'If you'd done the right thing in the first place, none of this would be necessary.'

'This? Your attempt at blackmail? You're blaming me?'

Impossible man! 'Blackmail implies I'm doing something wrong. But right and the law are on my side. The crown is mine by right. Building a dam that will destroy so much of Edelforst is wrong.'

'Don't be so simplistic.' He shook his head and, in the first gesture she'd seen that revealed weakness or perhaps tiredness, he raked his fingers through his dark hair. Infuriatingly it fell perfectly back into place. 'You can't see the bigger picture. Some land will be inundated but the owners will be compensated handsomely. We're seeking sustainable ways to create power. This hydroelectric project will bring huge benefits.'

'You sound just like your father.'

His head jerked back, making her wonder what the relationship had been between the two men.

A muscle in his jaw worked. 'You spoke to him about this?'

She snorted. 'Chance would be a fine thing. We tried, my grandmother and I. Along with numerous delegations. But he refused to meet anyone. All the projections we sent him, all the scientific studies, the petitions and detailed analysis... All we got was a vague assurance that all input would be considered. Then the announcement that the dam would go ahead exactly as planned, *for the public good.*'

'It can be hard to accept change but when there's a clear public benefit—'

'*Public* benefit? Are you serious?'

Her skin felt too tight to hold in her outrage. It felt as though ants crawled across her flesh. She wanted to leap up and stride around the room, waving her arms and releasing some of her pent-up emotions.

Instead she took a deep breath and looked out at the manicured formal gardens, seeking calm.

'You *have* read the documentation, haven't you? You know most of the power generated and the profits will go to private companies beyond our borders?'

'Only a percentage and only for a limited number of years. You can't expect them to help fund such a big project without getting some return.'

Annalena turned and met his steady gaze. Even now, in the privacy of the palace, he refused to admit the truth. The disparity between the press release he quoted and the true plans was vast.

She dragged in a shuddering breath. He was as brazen as his father, not even a hint of concern that he was selling out his people so others could profit. So *he* could profit.

Her shoulders slumped and she sagged in her seat. He was persisting in the lie his father had created.

She'd hoped a frank discussion would make him see the dam was a monumental error that would do environmental, social and economic damage. But there was no reasoning with a man who didn't see beyond the lining of his own pockets, for surely he'd get a cut of the profits.

Which meant her only hope was following through on her threat to wrest away the crown. She felt sick with dismay.

Annalena didn't want to swap her career for a life hemmed in by pomp and ceremony, especially since King Karl had tainted that world. She wasn't cut out for a royal life and feared she'd be overwhelmed as well as unprepared. Growing up with a title and a famous grandmother, she'd always been different to her peers. It had taken longer to make friends and be accepted. Some people still treated her differently. How much more isolating would it be as Queen?

Despite her fighting words earlier, she'd hoped this could be resolved simply. He'd tell her he'd changed his mind about the dam and she'd return home.

She couldn't give up without one last try.

'If you agreed not to proceed with the dam, and put it in writing, I'd consider signing away my rights to the crown.'

What was under that ground there that she so wanted to protect? Gold? Rare elements?

According to the summary Benedikt had read, the land was barely productive agriculturally and of little real value.

But to offer such a bargain...

She must have powerful reasons. To concoct a lie about being the true queen wasn't something to undertake lightly. And if by some million-to-one chance there was something in her claim, why agree to give it up for a dam?

He was missing something. Benedikt hated that feeling. He had a flair for business but most of his success came from hard work and attention to detail. He never allowed himself to be caught unprepared.

But Annalena of Edelforst had done just that. He felt as if she'd ripped the antique carpet out from beneath his feet and he'd suffered concussion from smashing his head on the floor.

In the hours since she'd flounced into the palace, he and Matthias had followed up her claim of royal lineage. He made a mental note to review the files for the dam project as soon as possible.

He'd only had time to read the summary report, because he was trying to get across so many things in a short time. His father had been selective about which royal matters he took on, keeping real power to himself, jealous even of his son who'd one day inherit. Now Benedikt paid the price for that.

'Do we have a deal?'

She had to be kidding. There'd be no deal of any kind until he knew exactly what was going on and why.

'I don't do deals with people who try to blackmail me.'

He had the satisfaction of seeing her eyes widen in dismay. A softer man might almost feel sorry for her.

Except she was trying to manipulate him, something he abhorred. His father had revelled in making people dance to his tune, playing on their vulnerabilities.

Was that what Annalena had attempted with her big, doe eyes? Making a production of eating that gateau as if it were a prelude to sex? The way she'd taken her time biting into it then chewing, eyes flickering half closed as if in sensual delight, then licking away crumbs from her sweetly curved mouth.

Heat eddied in his belly, drawing tight and low, provoking anger at how easily she affected him.

'My answer is no.'

She sat higher, fingers curling around the arms of her chair. Her mouth flattened, jaw tightening. And her eyes... they were slits of green fire, hot enough to scorch.

A childhood memory stirred. An old legend about the dragon that had haunted the high Alpine reaches of Prinzenberg. Not only could it breathe fire, but also turn to stone anyone foolish enough to meet its stare.

Benedikt breathed deeply, meeting that incendiary look. His pulse quickened as adrenaline pumped hard and he welcomed it, welcomed the surge of response. He told himself it was because, after months grappling with his father's convoluted backroom deals and half-truths, he found honest dislike refreshing.

Bizarrely, her searing look *was* turning him to stone.

His lower body was weighted and hard. That sizzling gaze was like a hand stroking his skin, reminding him how long it had been since...

There was a rustle of silk as she rose. 'In that case we're finished here. I have an appointment with a constitutional lawyer tomorrow.'

Benedikt stood too, closer than he'd intended. Close enough to feel her heat and inhale her light floral scent. 'Because you're giving up your claim?'

Her fiery stare turned cool. 'I didn't come here to walk away empty-handed.'

Unfortunate but predictable.

'Then you won't walk away.'

Her gaze searched his and he had an uncanny sense of familiarity. But they'd never met before. He'd only seen her at a distance once in his youth.

'Why are you looking at me like that?'

'You don't think you can drop that bombshell then stroll away?' Benedikt shook his head. 'Until the succession is clarified, you'll stay here.' His lips curved in a feral smile. 'As my guest.'

CHAPTER FOUR

'ARE YOU *THREATENING* ME?' Annalena hoped the quiver in her voice was anger.

He looked different, as if beneath his control lurked something untamed. His sharp smile contrasted with that heavy-lidded, almost lazy stare that she knew was anything but indolent. His tall frame almost hummed with energy.

'Of course not. Threat implies something unreasonable.' He folded his arms, making her even more aware of his height and the impressive breadth of his chest. 'I'm sure you'll agree I've been remarkably fair-minded in the circumstances.'

She considered reminding him it was *his* fault they'd got to this stage, by refusing to heed the information sent to him about the hydroelectric project. But a glance at that rigid jaw told her recriminations were pointless.

'Once the confusion about your arrival was cleared up, you've been treated courteously. I listened to your story. I set in motion enquiries to verify or disprove it.'

So he *had* taken action to confirm it. Annalena didn't know whether to be relieved or worried. Would his agents try to steal the original documents? Would they harass her grandmother?

'Meanwhile you've enjoyed my hospitality and the company of an old friend.'

'Only because you wanted to verify my identity.'

'That too.' He paused, his lowered eyebrows giving him a brooding look. Yet to her dismay even that didn't mar his dark charisma, a charisma she didn't want to notice. 'Given your allegations about my father, my behaviour has been remarkably restrained.'

A micro expression flitted across his features. Repudiation? Who would want to believe their father was a murderer? For a moment she felt a surge of sympathy.

Automatically she opened her mouth to apologise for any distress caused, then realised how absurd that was. The truth wasn't her fault and she wasn't broadcasting it publicly. She was giving him the opportunity to deal with this behind closed doors.

'Thank you for the meeting,' she said through gritted teeth. 'And the refreshments. But it's time I left. We can speak when you've completed your enquiries.'

She was turning away when he spoke. He didn't raise his voice. It was smooth, almost soft. 'You really think *that's* reasonable behaviour, Annalena?'

Something tickled her spine as he said her name. It felt like the caress of a feather, drawing her flesh tight and making her insides quiver.

Her hands fisted. 'You're accusing *me* of being unreasonable?'

That brooding stare locked on hers and she had the strangest sensation that she couldn't step away. Those intense eyes pinioned her. His gaze flicked to her mouth then her eyes and tension notched higher, a sense of *anticipation* unlike anything she'd experienced.

'You've spent a long time angry with my family, fixated on our apparent crimes. But consider this from my perspective. I was unaware of the issues you raised until today.' A muscle jerked in his jaw, making the harsh set of his features suddenly more human. 'The allegations are serious and I'll get to the bottom of them.'

'But—'

'If true, they have the potential to cause alarm, if not panic in a country already reeling from the unexpected death of its king. If true, they'd cause a constitutional crisis. In the circumstances, it's *sensible* for you to stay while we sort it out.'

She shook her head. 'I've already provided the documentation you need. But I don't need to stay here.'

She'd hated the palace, or what it represented, all her life. It had been home to the scheming criminal who'd killed her father and, she was convinced, her mother too. Oma had insisted her daughter had died from grief for her husband.

Annalena's nemesis went on, his voice implacable. 'If you're really the Queen, you'll need to get used to living and working here.'

The idea shot a bolt of cold steel through her ribs.

No, that wouldn't happen.

She'd sign over her rights to the crown once the dam was stopped. She had no desire to be Queen. Her life was fulfilling. She had no aptitude for court politics and no desire to learn.

'Meanwhile, having you here will be more efficient. I want this sorted quickly, don't you?'

'Naturally. But I can stay elsewhere in the city while you do that.'

That had been her plan, to visit the university and spend a few days catching up with colleagues.

'What are you afraid of, Princess?'

She wanted to tell him she didn't use her title and preferred he didn't, since he made it sound like a challenge. As if he thought her unworthy of it.

More, she wanted to scoff at the suggestion she was afraid. She was a competent professional, respected by her peers and the people of Edelforst.

Yet coming here into the lion's den was more daunting than she wanted to admit.

This was a world she'd avoided. Where his poisonous father had ruled, backed up by cronies who either couldn't see or didn't care how flawed he was. She'd rather be safely back home, surrounded by her work and her friends.

Annalena sucked in a shocked breath. Maybe she and her beloved Oma had more in common than she'd suspected. The old lady was as sharp and indefatigable as ever, but her physical world had gradually narrowed so she found it hard to leave home. That was why Annalena had come alone today. The Grand Duchess rarely left her castle and then only to visit familiar, nearby places.

'Princess?'

How she detested that casually raised eyebrow and mocking tone. As if this stranger sensed the trepidation she'd barely been aware of herself.

He didn't know the first thing about her. He was prodding, pushing her into agreeing.

It was infuriating that it worked. If she stayed she could negotiate the deal Edelforst needed and it would be finished all the sooner.

Besides, reading the glint in his eyes, she suspected if she didn't accept his hospitality he'd lock her in. He could make her his prisoner rather than a guest. Would he dare?

Despite his courtesy, she sensed his deep-seated implacability. Did she want to test it when, in the end, they'd have to negotiate?

She exhaled, forcing out the tension behind her ribs. Slowly she lifted her chin to meet his stare.

'Very well. I'll accept your *gracious* invitation.'

Her voice dripped disdain. They both knew there'd been nothing gracious about his words nor had there been an invitation, merely an ultimatum.

For a second she thought she saw the hint of a flush across his cheekbones but of course it was imagination.

Benedikt strode down the corridors towards his office. He knew he was scowling, jaw clenched, yet couldn't yet mask his discontent. The few staff members he met scurried out of his way.

Great. They probably thought the honeymoon period with their new monarch was over and he was reverting to type. His father's type. King Karl had been renowned for his bad temper when things didn't go his way.

That was enough for Benedikt to rein in his anger. In his darker moments he'd recognised his father's influence, his early years learning about the world and relationships from a ruthless narcissist.

He was lucky the old man had grown bored with parenthood so increasingly Benedikt had been raised by his mother. Karl had mainly intervened to interrogate his son on his learning, set impossible goals, and chastise his failures. Or use him as a hostage to the Queen's compliance, ensuring she acted the devoted consort even when their marriage broke down.

Eventually Benedikt had been allowed to summer each year in the US when his mother vacationed there, visiting her father. Without that Benedikt might have grown as monstrous as Karl.

Away from the palace he'd learned right from wrong and how to control his impulses rather than reach out and take.

But it hadn't been easy and even now he sometimes had to step back and consider his decisions.

Benedikt slowed, doing his best at least to look unperturbed.

Technically he'd got what he needed. Annalena was here where he could keep an eye on her. Where she couldn't get up to more mischief before this crisis was resolved.

But the woman had an uncanny ability to make him lose his cool. He'd had a lifetime to learn to mask his thoughts and feelings because his father had always played on emotions and weakness to his advantage.

With this one woman Benedikt felt too much.

He couldn't pin her down, alternately thinking her a liar or deluded. *Surely* her allegation about his father was untrue. As for the secret marriage, that must be a romantic fable concocted by her grandmother.

Yet something about the Princess Annalena had an authentic ring. A reluctant laugh huffed out. Even dressed like a milkmaid, she had more imperiousness in her little finger than some monarchs he'd met.

And charm too, when she chose to use it. He'd seen her with Colonel Ditmar and felt jealous of the old man. That smile…

Despite her wince when he called her Princess, she had the hauteur that came from a blue-blooded pedigree. She'd made him feel like an oaf though he'd been raised as Crown Prince.

She'd reminded him that he hadn't invited her to stay, but ordered it. As if he were his father's son in the worst possible way.

She was right. In that moment you'd happily have ordered security to stop her leaving.

Because they needed secrecy until this was sorted.

Or did the need to make her stay say something about his disturbing reaction to her?

Benedikt raked his hand across his scalp. He didn't have time for *reactions* to any woman.

Having her here was necessary. He needed to control the spread of her preposterous story until he could disprove it.

Yet you didn't confiscate her phone. It would only take one call from her to the press.

No matter how tempting that had been, he was determined to prove himself different to his father. He was a fair-minded man, not a tyrant, even if he was determined to take control of this situation. Besides, if she'd planned to wreak immediate chaos, she'd have done that already.

He couldn't work her out. She demanded he take her claims seriously, yet in the next breath talked about giving up the crown if he'd stop the dam.

Surely that proved this was a scam. How many people would give up the chance for wealth and royal privilege?

Despite his difficulties untangling his father's more dubious arrangements, and reminding palace staff that they worked for the people as much as the King, there was no denying there were benefits to being ruler.

He entered his office, walked through to Matthias's desk in the next room and propped his hip against the desk. 'Any news?'

'Nothing conclusive. Sorry.' Matthias leaned back in his seat. 'The Grand Duchess and her lady-in-waiting will be interviewed tomorrow and I've arranged for an expert to view the original documents.'

'An expert?'

'Someone who knows about fraudulent documents. The police and courts have used him.'

'And the Grand Duchess is happy about that?'

'Very happy. Which makes me wonder. If it were all a hoax…' His troubled gaze met Benedikt's. 'Her only condition is that the documents be examined in her presence. And that if there's still any doubt about them, they be transported by someone of her choosing, who will remain with them throughout the whole process.'

Benedikt stiffened. 'She's implying *we* might do something nefarious with the papers!'

Matthias's expression was solemn. 'As if she doesn't trust you.'

'Which would make sense if her claims were true. Maybe she thinks I'm like my father.' A nasty premonition stirred in Benedikt's gut. 'Any news on the car accident?'

'Only the summary is digitised and it doesn't say much. Accident due to reckless driving. I've requested the physical files. But I did track down someone who was there soon after the crash. They were nervous about speaking but eventually confirmed a significant oil spill right across the road.'

'Which doesn't tally with the official report.'

'No, but there could be an explanation. We can't jump to conclusions.'

Yet Benedikt's thoughts turned irresistibly to the implications if this were all true. If the well-being of the nation rested on the narrow shoulders of a woman with no experience of government. Who, he'd discovered from Matthias's digging, made a living researching plants.

How useful would botany be in the complex work of managing a government? In dragging Prinzenberg out of the shadows cast by his father and into a more equitable, prosperous future?

A shiver ran down his backbone. It wouldn't come to that. It couldn't.

The country needed someone with experience of gov-

ernment, international affairs, social issues and economics
for a start. Someone to bring the nation together. Who understood the royal court and politics. Whose education and
personal experience had been tailored to make them a suitable monarch.

It needed *him*.

Annalena paced the gravelled path through the topiary gardens, heading for the parklike grounds she'd seen from her
suite.

It had been over twenty-four hours since she'd arrived
at the palace and, apart from her restless hours trying to
sleep, she'd only been able to relax during a couple of walks
through the gardens.

Being in the open air, preferably in wilderness, had always been her go to in times of stress. At home she headed
for mountains and forests when she needed to clear her head.

No chance of doing that here. The palace was an opulent prison.

Her spacious suite, stuffed to the gills with ornate an-
tiques, was nevertheless extremely comfortable. Nothing
was too much trouble, including sumptuous meals worthy
of a fine restaurant, which she'd eaten in stately solitude
in her private sitting room. Benedikt had excused himself,
saying he had to work, presumably frantically trying to disprove her story.

But she was aware of eyes on her whenever she ventured
from her suite. Whenever she opened her door there was an
usher at the end of the hall, ready to assist. Though those
ushers looked more like security staff.

To stop her leaving?

Her case had been collected from her car and brought to
her suite. She'd have preferred to get it herself, to enjoy the

freedom of being beyond the palace perimeter for a few minutes, but Benedikt had insisted.

Annalena wasn't fooled. He wanted her where he could
keep an eye on her. He'd even suggested that instead of visiting the university today she stay close, to be available for
any clarifications he required.

She could have insisted but hadn't wanted to press him
into a corner. It was easier to accede to a reasonable request
than force him to reveal his true colours. That could mean
armed guards barring her from leaving.

At least now you can pretend you're a welcome guest.

Despite the tension cramping her neck and shoulders, she
snickered. He probably feared she'd tell her story to a re-
porter. As if she wanted the world to know!

Nothing could be further from the truth. Annalena had a
fascinating, satisfying career, friends, and a home she loved
in Edelforst.

Coming to the capital, bearding the beast in his palatial
lair, had been a desperate last resort. Not an attempt to wrest
the crown from him.

Maybe if she'd been raised expecting to be Queen things
would be different. If she'd learnt about politics, government and economics, she'd have considered it. But while her
grandmother was a proud woman who hated that Annalena's
birthright had been stolen, she was a pragmatist and fiercely
protective. She'd seen what King Karl was capable of and
preferred to let her granddaughter build a life for herself,
safe from the threat of harm.

The bonds of love between granddaughter and grandmother were strong. That was why, when Annalena had rung
last night, she'd let the old lady believe she was staying in a
hotel as planned. No need to worry her with the news she'd
sleep under the enemy's roof.

Benedikt of Prinzenberg was used to command, having people obey. He was a quick thinker, powerful, and hated being crossed. Yet he wasn't completely like his father. His dismay when she'd spoken of murder had been genuine. She didn't fear for her life.

Yet he disturbed her in ways she couldn't name.

Being around him was like standing before an approaching thunderstorm. Everything felt charged and weighted with anticipation.

Annalena rubbed her hands up her arms as she left the formal gardens and stepped onto the springy turf of the private royal park. Ahead, a sweep of grass curved between stands of large trees to where afternoon sunlight glittered on a small lake.

She paused, inhaling the scent of growing things, then exhaling some of her tension.

Soon he'd have to acknowledge the truth and they'd come to an agreement. Then she could leave.

She didn't want to spend another night in his palace.

Down near the lake, they'd said.

What was she doing there, far from the palace buildings? Was this a tactic to make him come to her? To show she had the upper hand?

That would be petty and, despite the earthquake of disruption Annalena of Edelforst had caused, he didn't think her that.

Troublesome, yes.

Worrying.

An absolute disaster, for his country and everything Benedikt was trying to do here.

Yet despite the shockwaves still reverberating through him, not all his thoughts about Annalena were negative.

Because those thoughts don't come from your brain, but a more primitive part of your body.

Her combination of touch-me-not condescension and earnestness, not to mention a mouth created for kissing, kept distracting him. Her eyes flashed and her cheeks flushed when she spoke about the hydroelectric project and he'd wondered what else would excite her passion. *Who* else.

If she knew, would she use his distraction to her advantage?

She was here to negotiate, or said she was. A savvy negotiator turned any weakness to their advantage. He needed to do the same.

Benedikt paused by the water. She was nowhere in sight but must be close. Somewhere nearby security staff were keeping a discreet eye on her. They hadn't reported her trying to leave.

That was one positive at least. One positive out of a minefield of negatives.

He ploughed a hand through his hair. He couldn't believe how the day had unfolded. One after another, facts had been assembled and the truth he'd believed all his life distorted into something completely different.

But he didn't have the luxury of personal feelings. He had a nation to consider. That had to be his focus.

A sound caught his attention and he headed towards it, pine needles muffling his footsteps. He heard muttering then an off-key voice softly singing the refrain from a hard-rock anthem of a decade ago.

Benedikt paused. It couldn't be…

But he knew that voice. That husky, unmusical, but strangely beguiling voice belonged to the buttoned-up woman who threatened his country's peace and prosperity.

It made her seem approachable. Vulnerable. Not the keen-eyed competitor ready to rip the kingdom from his hands. Nor the foe whose femininity sidetracked him.

He stepped into the forest and there she was, squatting before a large tree, phone in hand, photographing something on the ground. The singing became a periodic hum as she shifted her weight, leaning in for a better picture.

Benedikt rocked back on his feet, taking in the view. She wore a T-shirt of dark khaki and jeans that clung taut against the curves of her backside, hips and thighs.

He swallowed and shifted his weight.

He must've made a noise because she swung round, twisting on the balls of her feet, her long ponytail flying across her shoulder.

There she was, the woman he'd seen on her driver's licence. Surprised but not uneasy, features alight. The set of her shoulders, the glow in her eyes and the curve of her lips told him she was happy.

Or had been until he'd appeared. He watched two tiny vertical lines appear above the bridge of her nose and her expression turn blank.

She rose in a fluid movement that spoke of fitness and agility. An instant later her phone had disappeared into a pocket and she stood, straight as a soldier on parade, facing him.

He found it unsettling.

Not that she should mask her emotions for this confrontation. But that he should mind.

Perversely, he wanted to know more about the woman who enjoyed grubbing on the forest floor and sang heavy-metal songs as they should only ever be sung in the shower. The woman who'd looked so joyful.

He'd like to know that woman.

'You were looking for me?'

'I didn't think I'd see you foraging in the leaf litter.'

It wasn't a criticism but she took it as one.

'I was told I had the freedom of the grounds.' She saw him taking in her appearance and pushed her shoulders back. Unfortunately that pushed her breasts against the fitted T-shirt and Benedikt had to work to keep his attention on her face. 'If I'd known we were meeting I'd have changed my clothes. I didn't pack for a stay in a palace.'

Benedikt smiled but his muscles felt stiff. Not just his facial muscles. 'That doesn't matter. I prefer casual.'

Her eyebrows rose as she surveyed his dark suit, white shirt and silk tie.

'I've come from the office. I've been working all day.'

Again he'd said the wrong thing, reminding her that she was filling in time instead of meeting colleagues at the university as she'd planned.

He looked past her to the red fungi she'd been photographing. Or perhaps it was the tuft of tiny white flowers beside them.

For a bizarre moment he wished he could question her about that, hear her talk about her work. He wanted to meet the light-hearted woman who found wild vegetation more fascinating than a grand baroque palace full of priceless art and heirlooms. Or, apparently, the chance to be Queen.

He wanted to engage with her without royal responsibility weighing him down.

He stifled the selfish urge. His country needed him to focus on resolving this problem, quickly!

Her gaze turned laser sharp as if she read his thoughts. Yet when she spoke she sounded wary, not eager. As if she didn't want to hear his news. 'You have news?'

'I do.' He watched her intently, trying to read any micro-expression. 'It seems you *do* have grounds to claim the crown of Prinzenberg.'

CHAPTER FIVE

ANNALENA FELT HER features freeze, like ice spreading across a mountain tarn in winter. She even heard the warning crackle of shifting ice beneath her feet, as if she'd stepped beyond the bounds of safety.

It took a second to realise the sound wasn't ice, but twigs cracking beneath her shoes as she instinctively backed up.

That made her stop and draw in much-needed oxygen.

There could be no retreat. No sign of vulnerability. Not while negotiating with Karl's son. He'd use weakness to his advantage.

This was what she needed. His admission was the first step to stopping the dam. To saving homes, jobs, habitats and people's way of life.

Yet being next in line for the throne was *so* not what she wanted, fate's joke at her expense.

Deep breaths. Now the negotiations begin. Now he knows the power in your hands he'll agree to your terms. It will be over soon.

She breathed out, willing her taut frame to relax. 'You admit I'm the rightful heir?'

His expression gave nothing away. What had she expected? A bitter rant? Threats?

Before she'd left home, she'd anticipated all that and more.

But once she'd met him, her expectations had altered. Despite his earlier antipathy, she'd never felt in physical danger as she would have with his father.

Benedikt was annoyed and authoritative but she couldn't believe he'd harm her. If she did, she'd never have stayed overnight. She'd have persuaded Colonel Ditmar to escort her out, or found another way to leave.

Or are you naive? You're in a secluded grove with a man you barely know and no witnesses.

Old nightmares brushed hoary fingers across her nape. Nightmares of the father she'd never known in a car that tumbled into an inferno at the bottom of a mountain.

A shudder racked her from the base of her skull to her heels, now planted wide on the ground.

'I admit that…' he paused as if reluctant to continue '…it appears possible. There are facts to be confirmed before we know for sure.'

Of course he wouldn't give in immediately. He'd hang onto power as long as possible. He mightn't be his father but he was a powerful man who didn't want to relinquish authority.

Annalena wanted to say she wasn't interested in taking it off him, but that was her bargaining chip. She had to stay firm until they reached agreement.

'How many people know?' she asked.

'Only those who need to.'

He shoved his hands in his trouser pockets, in the process pulling his jacket open to reveal a broad, hard-looking chest.

She blinked. He hadn't moved but that change of stance reminded her of their biological differences. He was taller and, by the look of it, fit. No doubt he was physically stronger.

She was sure he wouldn't harm her.

Yet you didn't tell Oma you were staying in the palace. You let her think you were in a hotel.

Because her grandmother had lived through the trauma of losing a beloved daughter and a son-in-law. Despite her fierce intelligence and iron will, that had changed her. Annalena hadn't wanted to worry her.

He asked, 'How many have *you* told?'

'None.' Before she could prevent them, more words spilled free. 'But my grandmother knows I'm here, and a lawyer has extra copies of the documents. If I don't return—'

Benedikt's oath was loud in the quiet grove. 'You think I'd harm you? You really believe…?'

She saw his disbelief, then his features settled in an outraged scowl before he turned and strode away. He reached the far side of the glade then spun back, his long paces eating up the distance, bringing him to a halt an arm's length away.

It felt closer. He all but crackled with energy. She felt it lift the fine hairs on her arms and nape, drawing her skin tight with goosebumps.

Eyes like molten metal held hers. It was like looking into a furnace, so bright it hurt.

'Whatever you believe about my father, whatever he may have done… I. Am. Not. Him.'

His chest rose mightily and she saw the frenetic beat of his pulse at his temple.

When he spoke again his voice was softer yet heavy with repressed emotion. 'I don't deliberately hurt people, Annalena. I won't harm you.'

She believed him. His horror at her words was real. She still felt the shock of it reverberating around them.

Annalena nodded. 'I know.'

'Do you? You take my word for it? Isn't that too trusting?'

An outsider might think so. She'd have thought so earlier. She didn't pretend to understand everything about him, but the man she was just beginning to know didn't fill her with dread.

On the contrary, he filled her with an uncomfortable feminine yearning stronger than she'd ever experienced.

Instead of wanting to shrink from him, she wanted to get close. It was one of the reasons she had to ground herself firmly whenever he was around. So as not to give in to temptation and get closer.

'I'm not saying we're on the same side. I'm not naive. But I believe you.'

He didn't look convinced. 'Yet you took precautions in case you disappeared.'

So she'd had a moment of uncertainty and fear. But her fear had more to do with her turbulent reaction to him than any true belief he'd harm her.

She lifted one stiff shoulder. 'I was going into battle. I couldn't take risks.'

Was that understanding in his gaze? 'Especially given what happened to your father.'

Her heart jolted. 'You believe now that it wasn't an accident?'

'I don't know. I doubt we'll ever know, given how much time has elapsed. But there are discrepancies in the reports.'

For the first time Annalena noticed lines of tiredness around his eyes, worry imprinted on his forehead and bracketing his mouth. She'd sensed yesterday that he wasn't close to his father. But to confront the possibility Karl had been a killer...

'Where do we go from here?'

His mouth kicked up at one corner, like a tick of approval. 'Charming as this place is, I vote we move to somewhere

ANNIE WEST 63

we can be more comfortable.' He gestured for her to walk with him. 'Shall we?'

Annalena cast a glance around the clearing. Personally, she'd rather have their discussion here. She found the palace oppressive. But admitting that would hand him an advantage. He mightn't want to harm her but she needed her wits for this negotiation.

A quarter of an hour later they entered a large walled garden. Unlike the topiary garden, this wasn't regimented. Paths meandered and there was a riot of colour from flowering trees, shrubs and annuals.

'Let's talk here,' she said impulsively. He paused mid-step, and she hurried on. 'Surely you've had enough indoor meetings?'

'Why not? I know just the place.'

He led her around a circular path to a summerhouse surrounded by scented, climbing roses in shades of cream, yellow and bronze. Opening the door, he invited her to precede him.

A few paces in Annalena stopped, breath catching. The octagonal room was filled with light from the many full-length windows, despite them being half obscured by roses.

White-painted furniture looked comfortable with an abundance of cushions in pastel gelato colours. The ceiling was wallpapered with a vivid print of a lavish garden from which peeped exotic birds and animals. Suspended from the ceiling was a chandelier, not antique crystal, but of glass in a multitude of colours, creating rainbows across the room.

The place was whimsical and welcoming and lifted her spirits. She'd never thought to see anything so delightful in the palace.

Between two windows was a tall cabinet crammed with books, drawing Annalena. The titles weren't organised alphabetically or by size but by some arcane logic, presumably known only to the owner. They seemed well read and most were about plants and gardening.

She swung around, taking in the lovingly tended pot plants. The small tables strategically placed beside the seats. She could imagine afternoons here with friends. Or curling up on that long sofa with books from the cabinet and a piece of cherry torte. It would be a cosy place to work on her laptop.

'This is marvellous! Just…perfect.'

In the doorway, Benedikt's expression was inscrutable. Finally he stepped inside, looking around as if he hadn't seen the place in a while. 'I'm glad there's one part of the palace you approve of.'

Apparently she hadn't hidden her dislike for the place well. 'I'm not really into gilding and formality.'

'You grew up in a castle. Your grandmother still lives there.'

She lifted one shoulder. 'Some of the rooms there are very grand but not all the spaces are formal. It's old and quirky and…comfortable.'

'And this palace isn't?' Before she could answer he continued. 'You don't have to be polite. No one in their right mind would call Prinzenberg's palace cosy.'

'But you have this. Whoever designed it knew how to create a welcoming, relaxing space.'

'My mother's talent. You should have seen our New York penthouse.'

'Your mother designed this?' Annalena looked around with new eyes. It couldn't be any more different to the parts of the palace she'd seen. 'She could have been a professional designer.'

'I agree. But it wasn't seen as compatible with her royal obligations.'

Annalena's gaze sharpened. Was he telling her a queen

wouldn't have time for another career? That if she took the throne, she'd have to give up her profession?

But his expression as he surveyed the room suggested he wasn't thinking of her.

She racked her brain for everything she could remember about the now dead Queen. An American who'd increasingly spent more time overseas than in Prinzenberg. She'd borne the King one live son and one stillborn. In the last few years before her death she'd appeared at the King's side only at a few key royal events.

Had she been unhappy? Was that why Benedikt looked pensive? Annalena had barely had time to adjust to the possibility when he turned that bright stare on her, sending heat arrowing through her body.

'We need to discuss the future.'

She nodded, subsiding gratefully into a chair. Time to finalise this.

Wary eyes met his. 'Have you looked at the material about the dam? It proves—'

'We'll talk about the dam soon. Our first priority is the crown.'

Benedikt watched her stiffen, the corners of her mouth crimping down.

'The issues are linked. I told you, if you kill the dam project, I won't press my case to be Queen.'

'Saving that valley means more to you than ruling the country? With all the wealth and influence that brings?'

If so, she was remarkable. Through the ages, all around the globe, people had struggled and connived, even killed to win a crown.

A vast chasm carved open his belly. Was that what his father had done? Killed for a crown?

He'd probably carry that suspicion for the rest of his life. Another weight to add to his already heavy burdens.

'Yes, it does mean more to me. There's no benefit to Edel-forst from the project, only destruction. The power gener-ated will be diverted elsewhere and so will the profits. There are better, more cost-effective ways of generating power than flooding the valley. We'd lose our heartland. We can't allow that.'

Was that a royal 'we'? With that spark in her eye and tone of condemnation, she was every inch the displeased monarch.

'What about the next project you don't like?'

Her brow knitted in confusion. 'I don't understand.'

'If the government decides on a future policy that affects your province, a policy you disagree with. What will you do?

'Bring forward our concerns, of course.'

'If that doesn't work and you lose the argument, what will you do then? Reassert your claim to the throne? Threaten a constitutional crisis to get your own way?'

'This isn't about *me*.'

Benedikt shook his head. 'It's absolutely about you. No matter what you say about altruistic motives, if it's proven you have a right to the throne, what's to stop you wielding that against me, or my heirs?'

'I'm not interested in being Queen.'

'But you *are* interested in what happens to Edelforst. Look how far you've gone to protect it.'

She opened her mouth then snapped it shut. 'I'll sign a document written by your lawyers, giving up my right to the throne, on condition—'

'Yes, I know. On condition the dam doesn't proceed.'

He'd heard more than enough about that. What he *needed* to sort out was whether he could legitimately rule Prinzenberg or be forced to hand it over to a woman who wasn't interested in it, and who had few if any of the skills to run it.

Not because she wasn't intelligent, but because she'd never learned. How long would it take a novice to come to grips with what he'd spent a lifetime learning? Especially with so many so-called advisers ready to lead her into decisions that would serve them rather than the country. Cronies who'd benefited from his father's rule and administrators with a vested interest in stifling public scrutiny.

Could Prinzenberg afford to wait years for her to catch up?

Benedikt thought of the problems he'd uncovered in just six weeks and knew they didn't have that much time.

He dragged in a sustaining breath. 'You could sign such a document. And I'm sure that at this moment you're convinced you'll abide by it. But if later you change your mind, *I'd* be the one facing the fallout.'

Her brow knotted. At least she hadn't jumped to contradict him.

'Look at it from my point of view. If it came to light later that you'd signed away your right to the throne to save your precious valley, it would seem like coercion. Maybe, technically, you'd be barred from taking the crown. But all hell would break loose. The people and the parliament could take sides. There'd be division and argument. Prinzenberg would be brought to its knees. It could take years to sort out.'

She sat stiffly, her eyes flashing pure green in her flushed face.

No wonder he'd thought her familiar yesterday. He'd believed he'd looked into that clear gaze before, and he had. But it wasn't Annalena's. The eyes he remembered belonged to Crown Prince Christian, the man whose death had ushered in his own father's rule. Those vibrant eyes looked down at Benedikt every time he passed the royal portraits on the way to his office.

She had her father's eyes.

If he'd still believed that right always won out, he'd be tempted to step away now. Let her have the crown while he pursued his own interests in America and elsewhere.

But Benedikt wasn't that unworldly. Living with his father, not to mention years in business and working for his country, had ensured that.

His country needed a strong monarch who'd protect and serve it well.

'You doubt my word?'

'I doubt that you fully understand the bomb you've primed to explode. Whether it's now or in the future, it *will* explode, unless we deal with it.'

'We can keep this secret. My grandmother kept the circumstances of my birth secret all these years.'

'Which is an extraordinary feat. But only a few, very loyal people knew.' He leaned forward, tempering his voice to hide his urgency. 'Think about what's happened since you came here. The people who have seen you and know you stayed here overnight. Administrative staff who are wondering why certain files have been requested. Only a hand-picked few have conducted interviews in Edelforst, but gossip will be circulating already.'

She slumped in her seat, eyes round. He had to make her understand.

'This is no longer about a very few, trusted people with your well-being at heart. It's gone beyond that. People will be curious and start digging. People who aren't necessarily loyal to me or you. People who learned under my father to use knowledge as a currency to win power for themselves.'

'Why do you keep them on?'

'I won't. But change takes time. I can't sack all his staff and advisers on the spot. I owe them the chance to prove themselves, or not. But my point is, we can't assume everything will be solved with your signature on a piece of paper. We have to prepare for a future when this secret may become public.'

He didn't mention the other possibility. That Annalena might change her mind down the track. What if she had a baby? Maternal instinct might prompt her to claim the throne for the sake of her child.

She stared into the distance, biting her bottom lip, and heat shafted to his groin.

His mouth firmed. He didn't need the distraction of sexual awareness on top of everything else. But it had been there from the moment she'd marched into his office and it wasn't fading. Seeing her in casual clothes, in something like her own environment, only heightened his response. As did her ignorance of or apparent lack of interest in her sexual allure.

How long since he'd met a woman like that? Even in college the women he'd met had been supremely conscious of their appearance and his reaction to them.

And that you were heir to a throne and a fortune.

Excitement tickled his backbone as he surveyed Annalena.

The sexual awareness wasn't one-sided. He'd seen the way her pupils dilated, her gaze on his mouth when he spoke. The way she leaned closer until she realised what she was doing and abruptly pulled back.

Yet she didn't care about his money or status. If anything, those counted against him.

That mutual attraction was the only positive he could see in this whole tangled mess. It would be useful when—

She shook her head, pink lips forming a moue of concentration that made him harden. How could he be susceptible to such an innocent expression?

'I can't see we have any other alternative but an agreement like I proposed.'

Benedikt took his time replying, tamping down his unsettling physical reaction.

He'd come up with an alternative and spent the night and all today testing its weaknesses. It would be difficult but not impossible. Unconventional, but so were the circumstances.

That fact that it was something he'd rather avoid was immaterial. It would be manipulative and ruthlessly efficient, but then wasn't he Karl's son? He swallowed bitterness that perhaps he'd inherited his father's conniving mindset after all.

'I have a solution. You'll get what you want for your province, no dam. I'll get security of tenure as King. And the country gets the stability and leadership it needs.' He paused. 'That's vital. It's not public knowledge and I don't want it to be, but Prinzenberg is facing serious problems. My father and his supporters stripped public assets for their own gain. There are other issues too that will take time to sort out.'

His heart thudded against his ribs. He hated sharing that but needed to make her understand the gravity of the situation.

This wasn't just about Annalena and Benedikt and their personal preferences. It was about the well-being of their homeland. He couldn't renege on that responsibility.

'And I thought it would be straightforward.' Her mouth twisted. 'What's your win-win solution?'

'Now you've opened this can of worms, we can't pretend it didn't happen. We have to move forward. We'll make the best of the situation, for everyone's sake.'

Her frowning stare met his. 'I get a bad feeling when you

don't give me a straight answer. What's so bad you have to cajole me into accepting it?'

Benedikt spread his hands, palms up in a gesture of openness to show he had no hidden agenda.

'My coronation goes ahead in a couple of weeks and you'll be at my side.' He watched her eyes widen. 'As my bride. We'll be crowned together.'

CHAPTER SIX

ANNALENA SHOT TO her feet and across the room. When she reached the window and spun around it was to find him on his feet, watching her.

Did he think she was going to make a run for it?

He had the determined look of a man ready to stop her.

She stifled a snort of despairing amusement. How could she run? She was as mired in this situation as he. All through their discussion she'd told herself there would be a way out. Surely they could control things so everything went back to the way it had been.

But she'd found herself agreeing with every point he made.

Except the last one.

A huff of gasping laughter escaped. She'd been right to worry. His solution wasn't merely bad. It was *catastrophic*.

She folded her arms across her heaving chest, holding in the rackety thud of her heart pounding against her ribs.

'That's preposterous.'

'It's logical.'

'Maybe to a robot that doesn't understand the nuances of people's lives. Not to a *person*.' She hefted another breath. 'It's inhuman.'

She stared at the man watching her so steadily. How could

he even *think* it possible? He looked totally unruffled. Had he no sensibility? No feelings?

Yet there it was again, the throb of awareness that made it seem as though they stood a mere breath apart instead of metres away. She experienced it each time they met. As if there were a link between them. Even his far-fetched suggestion hadn't dimmed it.

His eyes glowed as they locked on hers and suddenly the tight feeling in her chest and her rapid heartbeat weren't just about his outrageous idea.

No, he wasn't a robot. He wasn't unfeeling.

He was human and very, very male.

A twisting sensation started up in the vicinity of her womb.

A moment ago she'd been shocked. Now she was swamped by the certainty she was completely out of her depth with him.

Her head spun and she planted her feet wider.

'Actually, it's a very human solution.' His voice was low, almost intimate. 'We both have issues that need resolution. By combining our resources we solve both problems and do it amicably. Then we can move forward and so can our country. You love Edelforst but it's part of Prinzenberg and I assume you care what happens to the nation.'

'Marrying is a little more than combining our *resources*.' To her chagrin, heat climbed her throat and into her cheeks. 'You're talking about joining our lives.'

And your bodies. Don't forget that. He's not the sort of man to be satisfied with a paper marriage. And he'll want an heir to the throne.

That twisting ache low in her body intensified.

From the first she'd been aware of Benedikt's intense masculine charisma. It wasn't the aggressive, boisterous masculinity some men exuded. But he was a powerful, virile man, an intelligent man who challenged and intrigued her. She was always intensely aware of him, mind and body.

She wasn't gullible enough to think he was proposing a temporary arrangement. Royal marriages didn't work like that, especially when both husband and wife had claims to the throne.

His eyes narrowed. 'You have plans to spend your life with someone else? You have a fiancé? A partner?'

Her chin lifted. She'd bet he knew there was no such person in her life. As well as researching her birth and her right to the throne, his staff would have compiled a report on her.

'Not at the moment.' Not ever. Because there'd never seemed time with her family obligations and her career. The circumstances of her birth and her parents' deaths had impacted her ability to throw herself carelessly into romantic love. Deep in her psyche, love and tragedy were inextricably entwined. Was it any wonder she hadn't taken that risk yet? Wariness, even fear, had kept her from the possibility of an intimate relationship. 'That doesn't mean I won't meet someone right for me in the future.'

He lifted his shoulders, the lazy action emphasising the leashed power in his rangy form.

'Perhaps with time we could be the right person for each other. Successful matches don't always begin with romance.'

He was talking about a match for dynastic reasons. What about the personal? Finding someone to share your hopes and dreams, your fears and delights?

She'd never been hung up on dreams of white bridal dresses and confetti. But through her rather isolated childhood and adolescence she'd hankered for someone with whom she could share her life. Now, approaching thirty, that had solidified into a desire for family, a partner and maybe children. But above all someone who loved her for herself, not for what she could do for her country.

'What about you? Do you have a partner? A fiancée?'

She waited for his instant denial. And waited. Her eyes rounded.

For the first time since the conversation began, his gaze strayed away from her. 'I—'

'You have a long-term lover and you'd throw her over without a second thought? Just to shore up your position?' Annalena backed a step and found herself pressed against the French door, hands splayed against glass. 'How could you—?'

'It's not like that.' He dragged his fingers through his hair, then, as if realising the gesture betrayed emotion, pushed his hands into his trouser pockets.

She stalked across the room to stand before him. She wanted to be close enough to read every nuance of his expression. 'What is it like, then, *Benedikt*?'

Annalena dropped her voice on his name, allowing him to hear the ponderous weight of her distrust and disapproval.

A muscle flicked in his jaw and he rolled his shoulders, standing taller. 'There's no partner, but I *have* been thinking about marriage.'

Surely the two went together. 'I don't understand.'

'Isn't it obvious? I've been considering potential brides. Someone to share the burden of royalty.'

Considering potential brides. He didn't sound happy about it. Did he have a list of requirements? Did he interview candidates? Or did he delegate that to his staff?

No doubt every woman on his list was gorgeous, talented and would make an admirable royal hostess. She'd have to be sexy too. Annalena couldn't imagine him accepting anything less. Especially as sharing the burdens of royalty no doubt included producing an heir.

Swallowing an acid taste, she asked, 'You have someone particular in mind?'

A brief pause before he nodded. 'But there was no agreement, no proposal.'

Annalena shook her head, folding her arms across her chest. 'Oh, that's all right, then. If there was no *agreement*.' Her lip curled. 'You've led her on to believe—'

'Marriage hasn't been mentioned. I haven't led her on.'

Did he really believe that? He must know the effect he had on women. If he'd been seeing her seriously he must have raised expectations.

Benedikt was well-built and imposingly tall with even— okay, handsome—features. Charismatic. Not to mention rich and royal. She suspected he merely had to smile at a woman to raise her hopes.

Unless that woman was clear-eyed enough to recognise his autocratic tendencies. His unyielding drive to get what he wanted. How else could you describe his idea of them marrying?

Cold-blooded, that was what he was. Even if he made her feel hot and bothered.

His gaze snared hers and held it. And despite her distaste for what he was doing, she felt that frisson of awareness, not just of him, but of herself. The heat under her skin, the weight of her breasts against her lace bra and an achy emptiness in her pelvis.

'It's true. I take my duty seriously and that includes choosing a queen. I was in no rush. The woman in question and I know each other but that's all. No promises were made.'

Just how well did they know each other? It wasn't any of Annalena's business, but she couldn't help wondering.

That worried her. *He* worried her.

Their interactions had been fraught with tension and distrust. Yet there'd been brief moments of something like communion, as when they'd entered this room. And too many other moments when she'd thought of him as a man instead of an opponent.

He messed with her head and she knew it wasn't all intentional. Much of the time she sabotaged herself with her wayward thoughts. Her mind strayed to last night's restless sleep and those disturbing dreams, all featuring Benedikt. And he hadn't always been so formally dressed.

Her gaze skittered away.

'Even so, it wouldn't work. I couldn't marry a man I can't respect.' In her peripheral vision she saw his head rock back. 'Not even for my country.'

'I told you, I'm not my father.'

His voice was colourless, the deliberate absence of emotion making her nerves jangle. Because only someone suppressing every emotion could sound so barren.

She looked back at him. Sure enough, despite his stillness, she saw traces of anger and wounded pride in his strong features.

'Yet, even knowing how disastrous that hydroelectric project will be, you didn't stop it when you came to power. You ignored all the evidence that proves it's a mistake. Do you have a personal financial interest in it too?'

Benedikt didn't step closer but his deep breath lifted his shoulders, expanding his chest, making her more aware than ever that she faced a formidable adversary. She felt a jitter of nerves but stood her ground.

'That project is one of many. Until yesterday I hadn't dug deeply into it. I'd accepted that a full feasibility study had been completed.' As if anticipating her protest, he raised his hand. 'Last night I read all the files. The only material there fully supports the benefits of the project. There's no record of representations against the scheme. No other studies, no petitions, nothing.'

'What?' She moved closer, as if proximity could force the truth. 'They have to be there.'

He shook his head, and this close, his expression looked more like regret than anger. 'I read it all and my personal staff double-checked every file. There's nothing negative except an acknowledgement of losses by a few farmers, and a plan to recompense them generously for losing their land.'

Annalena gaped. 'I *knew* the process was rigged. But this...!' It was inconceivable. 'How could they *do* that?'

'My father didn't like dissent, particularly when he'd already made up his mind.'

Benedikt's expression was so grim it cut through her fury. What had it been like, growing up with a father like that?

Worse than growing up fatherless.

He spoke again. 'I'm rapidly learning how deeply that's affected the administration here. I suspect that to keep their jobs, staff learnt to tell him only what he wanted to hear.'

'To the point of falsifying public records?'

'So it seems.' For a moment he was silent. 'The next ruler will have plenty to deal with.'

There was deliberate provocation in the way he watched her. As if daring her to reassert her claim to the throne. Almost as if he'd like her to take it. But that couldn't be.

More to the point, did she believe that he hadn't been part of this corrupt plan?

Her position would be much easier if she doubted his word. The trouble was that she couldn't typecast him as a villain. He was so angry and resentful about what his father had done. And looked serious about the task ahead to make things right.

'So you're not pro-dam?'

'Not if the evidence proves it's a bad idea.'

'I can get you that evidence today.'

Her fingers itched to reach for her phone but now wasn't the time. He was right, there was more at stake than a single infrastructure project.

'Do that. Nothing will proceed until it's reassessed.'

Relief was a mass of butterflies in her stomach. 'Once you have proof of the true situation you'll stop the project.'

She made it a statement, not a question.

Yet instead of agreeing, he stepped up to her, making her pulse thrum and her breath catch.

'I could say the same to you, Annalena. You know the precarious situation created by your claim to the throne. Unless it's settled definitively the country faces a possible power vacuum and uncertainty in all levels of government. That could take ages to sort out. Just when we need stability and good leadership more than ever.' He leaned close and the air between them fizzed with energy. 'If you're as principled as you imply, you'll do your part to rectify that once and for all.'

She swallowed, almost choking on the knot of dismay clogging her throat.

'By marrying you.'

Her tone was supposed to be scoffing. Instead it was a raw whisper. But he heard it. How could he not when he stood so close that his body heat made her temperature spike?

'Exactly.'

What worried her most wasn't that he looked triumphant or smug. He didn't. This wasn't the expression of a man who *wanted* to marry her. He looked determined and expectant.

Her brain whirled with all the reasons marriage was impossible. But every objection she could raise faded before the need to put her country first.

And he knew it. She saw it in his eyes.

Her upbringing had centred around duty. To family, to her people, to Edelforst, and yes, to Prinzenberg.

From a child she'd learned to put others first. Her grandmother had seen to that and had provided a strong role model, counselling, leading and representing her people for decades.

Annalena had always known at some point in the future she'd carry on that role after her grandmother. That was why she'd come here.

But not to marry a stranger!

'There must be another option.'

The lift of one dark eyebrow told her what Benedikt thought of that. 'If you can come up with a better solution, let me know.'

He didn't look any more impressed by the idea than she was. After all, he'd already chosen a suitable bride. He didn't want Annalena any more than she wanted to tie herself to him.

Maybe she could use that to her advantage.

'Marriage between us wouldn't work.'

'We'd make it work.'

Annalena looked away. 'We're not compatible. That would make for a very uncomfortable marriage. *And* everyone would see through the sham of it once we were in the spotlight together. The days are long gone when royals marry solely for dynastic reasons.'

'Not compatible?'

His voice held a note she couldn't identify, but it made her turn to meet his stare.

Instead of looking argumentative, his expression was even blanker than before. As if he couldn't even be bothered to argue the point. Those brief moments of connection she'd felt earlier must have been in her head.

That bland stare riled her.

Once or twice, early in her career, male colleagues had tried to blank her, pretending her input wasn't as valuable as theirs. They'd attempted to undermine her confidence and others' belief in her. It didn't happen any more because she refused to be put down.

Her hands found her hips as she stared into Benedikt's strong features. And noticed again how disturbingly good-looking he was.

Her pulse quickened in self-castigation.

'Exactly. Not compatible. Not attracted.'

It was only a partial lie. She might be strangely drawn to him but he'd given no indication he felt the same way about her. These inconvenient feelings were one-sided. The gleam she'd seen in his remarkable eyes was impatience, not attraction.

For the longest time he said nothing. Annalena was about to turn on her heel and head into the palace when he said, 'I disagree.'

Just that. As if his opinion were all that counted.

Maybe he was like his father after all.

She shrugged. 'There's no point discussing this any further. I'll—'

'It wasn't discussion I had in mind.' His voice dropped to a low burring note that rolled across her skin, making the fine hairs on her arms lift.

'Sorry?'

Suddenly he seemed much closer, though she hadn't noticed him move. 'No need to be sorry.'

Annalena frowned. It hadn't been meant as an apology.

'Can't you feel it?'

Now he *did* move nearer. Their feet almost touched and his breath warmed her face. To her dismay that made a decadent little shiver unfurl down her spine.

Light sparked in his eyes and she caught once more the glimmer of gold in dark brown irises.

Something whispered through her. A warning? An invitation? Whatever it was, it evoked a strange quiver in her stomach. She swallowed. 'Feel what?'

His head tilted closer, as if he wanted to read every nuance of her expression.

Not, absolutely *not* to kiss her.

Even so her heartbeat became a rapid flurry, as when lazy flakes of snow turned into a sudden blizzard.

Her nostrils flared as she detected an intriguing scent. It reminded her of verdant forests and crisp mountain air with a warm undertone of virile male. She inhaled deeply, drawing it in and feeling something tight in her chest give way.

Her brain blared an alarm but her body didn't notice.

She leaned in, chin rising, as if inviting him to close the space between them.

The realisation shuddered through her and she snapped her head back. She was about to move away when his hand closed on her shoulder.

His grip wasn't hard. She could step free, if she wanted to.

But there was something about the touch of those hard fingers through the cotton of her T-shirt that made her want to stay.

'This. Between us. It's been there from the first.'

An automatic denial formed in her head. She'd seen his initial reaction to her and it wasn't attraction. He was just pretending to make a point. But despite knowing that, her objection didn't make it to her tongue. Because, even understanding this was one-upmanship, she couldn't bring herself to stop it.

Another little tremor down her spine, through her legs and right to the soles of her feet.

That golden gaze dipped to her mouth and the beat of her blood turned to a roar in her ears. Her lips parted so she could suck in more air.

His eyes lifted to hers and the world telescoped so there was just him. Him and her. Every sense clamoured and her toes curled as awareness stirred.

Softly, so gently she thought at first she'd imagined it, something stroked her cheek. She caught a glimpse of his raised hand and his finger skimmed from her cheekbone to her chin, creating warmth deep in her body.

She had to break free. Now.

Resolute, she grabbed his wrist and pulled his hand away just as he leaned closer. Her breath snatched as his heat engulfed her. Wide shoulders filled her vision and gleaming golden-brown eyes fixed on her mouth as he brought his face to hers.

Annalena told herself to step back but was transfixed, waiting for the moment his mouth touched hers.

Surely one moment of curiosity was allowed? One moment before sanity returned.

He was so near her vision blurred, her eyes fluttering closed.

The moment stretched, her every sense on alert.

But when his mouth touched her it wasn't on the lips. She felt his mouth caress her earlobe as he whispered, 'Actually, we're *very* compatible. Attuned, even.' His voice was a rumble that turned her insides to a quivering mess and her knees to jelly. 'You're shaking in anticipation, did you know? If you'd just relax…'

'What? You'd seduce me in your summerhouse?'

Her nails dug into his wrist as she flung his hand away and stepped back. Eyes snapping open, she saw him blink, his expression for a second almost confused as he straightened to his full height. Her one consolation was that he looked almost as dazed as she felt.

But Annalena couldn't let that show. Desperately she reined in her anger, knowing if he saw it he'd realise it had its roots in disappointment.

He'd be right. She'd felt the drag of attraction from the first, while he'd felt *nothing*. He was playing on her weakness.

She thrust her shoulders back, hoping he wouldn't notice the way her nipples had hardened.

A lifetime concealing feelings behind a smile came to her rescue. Yet she didn't trust herself to meet his eyes. Instead she focused on the tiny scar above his left cheek.

'I'd rather you didn't practise your wiles on me, Benedikt.' She dragged air into too-tight lungs. 'This situation is hard enough without pretending attraction that's not there.'

'Annalena—'

'Let's talk later. I've had enough for now.' She turned and strode out the door.

CHAPTER SEVEN

'IT'S COMPLETELY OUTRAGEOUS,' Annalena repeated into the phone as she stared at the dusk-darkened gardens.

She wished she could be anywhere else but she couldn't leave until she and Benedikt came to some agreement. So she'd turned to her grandmother and they'd discussed the situation at length. It had been a relief talking to Oma. She'd been sympathetic and supportive. Unfortunately she hadn't been able to suggest a way out of this mess.

'Actually,' Oma said, after a long silence, 'in some ways it's an elegant solution, to have you share the throne.'

'Oma! How can you say that? It's horrible and—'

'I know, I know. I was obviously wrong about him, my information was flawed. He's an appalling man and you hate him. But then he's Karl's son. The apple doesn't fall far from the tree and if the tree's rotten…'

Annalena bit her lip then forced the words out. 'He's not like that. I don't like him but he's not like his father. He seems genuinely concerned about the country, for one thing.'

'Ah.' There was a wealth of meaning in that single syllable. 'You don't hate him after all.'

'Just because I don't think he'd kill for the throne, doesn't mean I *like* him. He's the most arrogant, infuriating man. He even tried to convince me—'

'Convince you of what?'

'Nothing important. It doesn't matter.'

Annalena was *not* going to admit how he'd undone her with the touch of his lips to her ear and the caress of his breath. That said more about her dormant love life than about him.

She shifted as that ache started up again deep inside. It had been there all day and every time she remembered those moments in the summerhouse she felt edgy all over again.

It was shaming. He'd merely been playing games while she'd reacted to him as if...

She cut off the thought, unwilling to go there.

'If you say so, darling. He's despicable but at least he knows his duty to the country.'

Annalena frowned. 'Despicable might be a bit too strong. But he thinks his way is the only way. He's too used to getting what he wants, particularly with women.'

'Ah, like that, is he? A puffed-up peacock. That's interesting. I'd heard he was actually quite sensible.'

Annalena didn't say anything. She supposed he *was* sensible, when it suited him. The way he'd outlined their situation had been compelling. But that didn't mean his conclusion was right.

'But he's wrong. There must be another way out of this.'

The silence lengthened and her tension grew.

When she was little her grandmother had always been there to comfort her, assuring her everything would be okay. But she wasn't a little girl now. She and her grandmother shared a relationship based on love but also honesty. Nowadays the Grand Duchess didn't soften the truth to make it more palatable. It was something Annalena admired, the old lady's determination to face problems.

Her silence now was a bad sign. Annalena had been so sure she'd have another option to offer.

'I'm afraid I agree with his analysis.' The old lady's tone made Annalena's stomach drop. 'He might be conceited but he's acutely aware of the pitfalls. This secret is growing too big. There's no guarantee we can keep it quiet. If it becomes public knowledge the fallout could be disastrous.' She sighed. 'I've lived through uncertain times. I don't want to see that again.'

Deflated, Annalena leaned against the window sill. 'But there must be an answer that doesn't involve marriage and me becoming Queen.'

Another silence, longer this time.

Sharp claws dug into Annalena's chest, dragging down, lower and lower. She drew in a shuddering breath.

'I'm not cut out to be Queen. I don't want to be.'

'We don't always get what we want, my darling.'

'You *want* this?'

She heard a drawn-out sigh. 'I'd hoped you'd find happiness. At the same time, this *is* your destiny. Your right and your duty. It's what your parents would have wanted, for you to rule the country.'

Annalena didn't know what to say. It was all well and good to talk about duty but this… Marrying a stranger! Taking a role for which she hadn't prepared.

'You know,' her grandmother said eventually, 'sometimes things aren't as they seem. Did I tell you how I met your grandfather?'

Annalena frowned at the ugly gilded clock on the other side of the room, her mind still on Benedikt and his proposition. 'I don't think you have.'

'Ah. I didn't like him you know, not at all.'

Annalena stiffened, shocked. 'That can't be. The way

you've always talked about him!' And it wasn't just what Oma had said but her tone and the soft light in her eyes when she spoke of her dead husband. Everyone knew the pair had been devoted.

'Oh, I *came* to love him. He was a wonderful man. But at first... Pfft. I thought him a pompous waste of space.'

An unwilling smile curved Annalena's mouth. 'Really? I can't imagine you giving such a man a chance to make a better impression.'

'That's just it. He was a visitor and I had to entertain him, though it was obvious my mother was matchmaking. It's a wonder he survived. I was sorely tempted to push him into the lake or over a cliff.'

'He can't have been that bad.'

'Well, no. As I eventually found out. But to begin with we rubbed each other the wrong way. Sparks flew whenever we were together. I found him completely infuriating. But first impressions aren't always right, my darling.' She paused. 'Maybe you should take a step back. Maybe your Benedikt isn't as bad as you think.'

He wasn't *her* Benedikt but Annalena saved her breath. There was no point protesting. Her grandmother's take on the situation was completely different to hers.

Soon after, Annalena said goodnight and ended the call.

Far from calming her, talking with Oma had unsettled her more. To the old lady, duty was a given. While she sympathised, she didn't view a royal marriage and coronation as a disaster. She'd probably be delighted to see her granddaughter as Queen.

Annalena frowned, rubbing her arms.

A wayward thought tickled her brain, stirred by the reference to matchmaking.

Had Oma suspected Annalena's trip to the capital might

lead to this debacle? Surely not. Even her canny grandmother couldn't have foreseen that.

Annalena stared into the night, wishing she could swap the floodlit gardens and city lights for her familiar view of mountain peaks.

Tomorrow she'd see Benedikt and he'd demand her answer. She *wanted* to say no. But this had gone far beyond what she wanted personally.

We rubbed each other the wrong way. Sparks flew whenever we were together. I found him completely infuriating.

Oma's words circled in her head. They were so apt, perfectly describing Annalena's situation.

Except for two things. First, her Oma had had the freedom to make up her own mind. Annalena's situation felt like a noose around her neck, tightening with each passing hour.

Second, what she and Benedikt felt for each other wasn't the beginnings of love. He was calculating and coldly pragmatic and she had no need for any man to tell her what to do. That moment of searing connection in the summerhouse, when she'd read something like hunger in his eyes, when the very air had felt charged with awareness—it had occurred *after* he decided he needed to marry her.

He wasn't interested in *her*, just what she represented. She wanted to save Edelforst and he, what did he want? It sounded as if he worried about the stability of the kingdom, yet, at the same time, was he like his father, driven by the need for personal gain?

They were mismatched. Even if their marriage benefited the kingdom, it would be a personal disaster.

'The Princess Annalena, sir.'

Frowning, Benedikt looked up from his desk. The fact the morning sky was still pink didn't bode well.

Annalena wouldn't visit at dawn to bring good news. Yesterday she'd looked at him as if he were something that slithered under the forest leaf litter.

That had stung, not least because he was used to attracting women, not repelling them.

His proposal might be unconventional but it was a perfect solution. How many generations had sealed a dynastic agreement with marriage? Though he'd rather avoid marriage, he told himself needs must, ignoring the cold shiver down his spine. His parents' marriage and the dysfunctional family in which he'd been raised had given him an aversion to marriage.

But a king needed an heir. He'd even started taking steps in that direction before this disaster blew up. Annalena's news just made the need to marry urgent.

Yet he recalled her horror when he'd suggested it and felt the spectre of his father stalking his conscience. Was he cornering her into marriage because beneath his lofty ideals he simply wanted the crown for himself?

He shoved his chair back, repelled by the idea. He was on his feet as she walked in and Matthias exited, closing the door.

She looked as if she hadn't had much more sleep than Benedikt. Yet the sight of her made his pulse quicken and his belly clench.

Because she held the security of the nation in her hands.

But it was more. This woman drew him in ways that had nothing to do with her claim to the throne. That, above all else, raised his hackles in wariness. He didn't have time for further complications. The situation was already convoluted enough.

'Won't you sit?' He rounded the desk and gestured towards a sofa.

Bright green eyes met his and his chest tightened.

Yet she wasn't trying to dazzle him. Again she wore casual clothes. Making a point that she wasn't impressed enough to dress up for him? Or because she hadn't planned to stay in the palace?

Jeans and a pale blue shirt that complemented her clear skin. In this place where everyone dressed formally, even behind the scenes, she was like a breath of fresh air.

'Thank you.'

She turned and took a seat and Benedikt had to wrench his gaze from the loving fit of denim against female curves and the supple sway of her hips.

'I wasn't sure you'd be in the office yet.'

Benedikt shrugged as he sat opposite her. 'I'm an early riser.' And sleep had been impossible. 'How did you sleep?'

Her eyes widened as if surprised. Annoyance stirred. Just how much of his father's reputation was she attributing to him? He felt like saying his mother had insisted on impeccable manners. That he wasn't an ogre who ate pretty little girls for breakfast.

Annalena shrugged. 'Not well. I had a lot on my mind. You?'

'The same.'

'What's so amusing?'

He hadn't realised he was smiling. 'In the short time we've known each other we've never beaten around the bush, have we? I appreciate that. I prefer unvarnished fact to polite untruths.'

'So do I.'

He believed it. Her reaction to his proposal had been forthright. His bruised ego was testament to that.

'I assume you're here to give me your answer.'

She inclined her head, her mouth pinching. 'Not that you actually asked.'

Benedikt frowned. 'I did you the courtesy of sharing the truth, Annalena. What is it you want? For me to get down on bended knee—?'

'No!' Her eyes rounded in horror. He couldn't decide whether it was because she wanted nothing to do with him, or because she didn't want to enact a farce. 'There's no need to insult us both with such a performance.'

Relief stirred, but so did annoyance. She had a unique ability to discomfort him.

'So you've made a decision.'

Her hands twisted in her lap before she saw him watching. Instantly she lifted her hands to the arms of her chair, adopting a pose that looked graceful and nonchalant. Except for the quickened pulse at her throat.

He liked it, he realised. The combination of outward serenity on a woman who, he'd learned, was volatile. Passionate.

Something stirred at the prospect of knowing her better.

Because, he realised, he *would* be knowing her better. If she planned to reject his proposal she wouldn't be jittery. Not that an ordinary observer would see her nerves. She pulled her collar close then sat straighter, the image of royal composure.

Inside him a tiny demon danced with glee. She was going to say yes.

'I *have* made a decision.' Her needle-sharp gaze skewered him. 'I'll accept the throne and marriage. With provisos.'

'Naturally.' He should have known she wouldn't make this straightforward. 'Go on.'

'I want your signature on a document stating that the dam

won't go ahead and I want your decision announced publicly, before the engagement is made public.'

'My decision?' he scoffed. 'Don't you mean *yours*?'

He'd yet to see the detailed argument against the project. Yet he couldn't fault her logic or her bargaining skills. He admired her for both.

'I'm happy to wait until you've read the papers. I sent them again to your office last night. In fact, take your time. I'm in no rush.'

'No. We'll finalise this quickly. And while we're talking about conditions, I have one. I want you to stay here until we announce the engagement.'

She blinked, pupils darkening the green of her eyes. Her skin paled. But instead of making her look fragile, the changes emphasised her allure and that elusive touch-me-not air.

Excitement stirred. She might have perfected the look but he'd learned her body sent a different message. Yesterday when they'd got close he'd felt her change from aloof to breathless anticipation.

Before Annalena's arrival he'd forced himself to consider marriage despite his own antipathy. Now though, he saw definite compensations.

'But I have work. Meetings. I can't just cancel everything.'

'It won't be for long. There's a grand ball at the end of the week, an official welcome to me as the incoming King. It will be a perfect opportunity to introduce you and announce our engagement.'

She shook her head. 'That's too soon.'

'The sooner the better. Your people in Edelforst will welcome an early resolution to the dam issue and there's no reason for us to delay, not with our coronation approaching so quickly. It's much better if people get used to the news in advance of the coronation.'

Annalena might have been carved from stone. She sat so still, as if she'd forgotten how to breathe. Yet when she spoke her tone was even.

'Do you have any idea how long it takes to create a ball gown, made to measure? Not only made-to-measure but spectacular? Because, believe me, only spectacular will do if you intend to announce our sudden engagement.'

He didn't, but that wasn't going to stop him. 'I'm sure there are any number of suppliers who'd move heaven and earth to fit you with a suitable dress in time. Designing for a queen would make their name.'

Her jaw worked. Was she grinding her teeth? Still her composure didn't crack. 'I can't persuade you to put off the coronation a little?'

'You assume correctly. The date is set. The only thing that will change is that it will be a double coronation and a wedding on the same day. It will make things much easier for us, for you, in the long term.'

He waited for the outburst but it didn't come. Instead she surveyed some point on the far side of the room. He could almost hear her brain working.

'Very well. I'll attend the ball but I can't stay here. At the very least I need to be visiting couturiers and—'

'No need. They'll come here. My staff will organise it this morning.'

Her head snapped around, her gaze fixing on his. He felt the sizzle of energy under his skin as if he'd been zapped by a live wire.

'An excellent idea.' Even white teeth bit off the word. 'But they can come to my home in Edelforst.'

Benedikt shook his head. He had no intention of allowing her off the premises until this deal was sealed. Not just with a marriage contract but with a public announcement so she couldn't back out. He needed to control the information around her right to the crown and their agreement until everything was settled.

He'd have security bar the palace exits if need be. But that would only cause fuss and bother. Annalena would be outraged and storm at him. He'd rather channel her energies into more productive directions.

'Time is of the essence, Annalena, remember? If you're here for fittings we'll make the deadline. If everyone has to traipse into the provinces...' He shrugged and spread his hands. 'Besides, a couple of days in the palace means you'll be available to sign relevant documents. You can get up to speed on any unfamiliar royal protocol. Better to be prepared, don't you agree?'

'I could still be available if I stayed in a hotel.' She paused, one eyebrow arching. 'Or don't you trust me out of your sight?'

Benedikt silently cursed. He'd promised honesty. 'Would you, if our situations were reversed? Would you trust *me*?'

Her gaze flickered. Her mouth tucked in at the corners as if suppressing disapproval or disappointment.

She rose in one graceful movement. 'Very well. I'll stay until the ball. But the morning after, I go home.'

She waited long enough to see him nod then swept from the room.

Benedikt was torn between relief and admiration.

Already she looked and acted every inch the Queen. He suspected she had the makings of an excellent ruler. For all her unpredictability and lack of training, she was focused on the public good, not herself. She listened, even when she didn't want to hear unpalatable truths.

Marrying her had been an impulsive idea, triggered by bizarre circumstances. But it was one of his best.

The question was whether he could break through her wall of disdain so they could forge a workable marriage. A mutually…acceptable marriage.

Another challenge to add to the long list, Benno.

Along with turning around a failing administration, rooting out corruption, announcing a betrothal that would stun the world and taking on the burden of ruling a country that had begun to lose faith in its leadership.

He had to win over the most determined, proud, distrustful, *distracting* woman he'd ever met and persuade her he wasn't some sort of Bluebeard. Easy!

He raked his hand through his hair and closed his eyes, ignoring the ache pounding at the back of his skull. He'd always liked a challenge but this…

CHAPTER EIGHT

'MADAM, MAY WE come in? His Majesty sent us.'

There was a sharp rap on the door to Annalena's suite but before she could reach it, the door opened.

She met a familiar, assessing gaze. It was less dismissive today yet she couldn't see anything akin to respect there. It was the woman who, a bare couple of days before, had tried to evict her from the palace. The woman who hadn't passed on the news that Annalena was waiting to see the King.

Unless Benedikt was lying and he'd known she was there all along.

It was profitless to ponder that now. In time she'd uncover the truth, when she had more than instinct to guide her. The man's actions would speak for his character.

'Madam?' From the threshold, impatience coloured the woman's tone. As if she had every right to intrude without invitation.

Annalena spoke into her phone. 'I'm sorry. The people I was expecting have arrived early. I'll call back later.'

She ended the call and walked to the door, rather than call across the vast room.

Her visitor looked sleek and self-important, again in a tightly tailored skirt and jacket, another silk shirt and high heels. Making Annalena aware of her jeans and casual shirt.

'You have the advantage of me. Clearly you know who I am but I don't know who you are.'

It was time someone taught the woman manners.

Annalena saw her eyes widen then narrow speculatively, and wondered at her attitude. Was she such a favourite she thought she could get by without common courtesy?

She *was* beautiful with her dark eyes and striking bone structure.

Was she a favourite of Benedikt's? Could that explain her arrogance?

Annalena tasted bitterness on her tongue.

No, he might be manipulative but surely he wasn't crass enough to make her deal with his mistress.

'Ida Becker, madam. I work for His Majesty.'

Did Annalena imagine the woman's taut expression softened as she mentioned him? She swung her gaze beyond her visitor's shoulder. 'Please come in.'

Annalena positioned herself beside the door, greeting the dress designer and her staff who followed, wheeling in rack after tall rack of gowns.

The sight of them filled her with dread. In only a few days she'd attend her first royal ball. At which time her engagement would be proclaimed.

After that there'd be no escape.

She could hear her Oma's voice in her head, talking about duty.

Her stomach churned, nausea stirring, until she sensed all eyes on her and turned, a serene mask firmly in place.

For the next fifteen minutes the discussion was all about the ball, Annalena's colouring and dress styles. She found herself saying less and less, which didn't seem to matter as everyone else had opinions.

The fact was she didn't know anything about formal ball gowns. Technically she might be a princess and, yes, Oma had insisted she learn to dance gracefully, but she'd never been to a ball. The glamorous events her grandparents hosted had ended with the death of their only child. As for attending regal events in the capital, the family had avoided them from that date.

Annalena knew how to dress well for conferences and civic events in what she thought of as business formal. Or wear traditional clothes for festivals. But a full-length ball gown? She'd never needed one.

For the first time she wished she'd spent less time researching botany and a little time pondering fashion. Could she pull this off and not look like the country bumpkin she suddenly felt? How many would be waiting, after Benedikt made his announcement, to see her fail?

'How about something like this?'

Ida Becker held out a long dress's voluminous skirt that seemed to consist of puffy tulle flowers. Annalena thought instantly of an oversized meringue. Worse, while some yellows worked for her, others, like this, would make her look jaundiced.

Annalena surveyed the woman's blank expression. Did Ida have no eye for colour, or was she trying to sabotage her? If so, why? Once more, Benedikt's name came to mind.

Before Annalena could object to the dress, the designer did. She shook her head emphatically and requested that Ms Becker stop fingering the delicate fabric, so crisply that Annalena had to stifle a smile.

Then the woman turned to her. 'Now, madam, if you'll permit, we need to take your measurements. If you wouldn't mind stripping to your underwear.'

Four sets of eyes scrutinised her and she felt a flicker of nerves. The last time she'd undressed before a stranger was when her grandmother had insisted she be fitted for her first bra, an experience she'd never wanted to repeat.

Annalena rose and reached for her shirt's top button. 'Thank you, Ms Becker, that will be all.'

'But—'

'I'll call if you're needed.'

By the time she'd finished unbuttoning, Ida had left, the door closing hard behind her.

'Sensible decision,' the designer said. 'She obviously has no idea what suits you. Why she thought she could add anything useful I don't know.' She clicked her fingers and one of the assistants scurried forward with a tape measure. 'Now, let's begin.'

'Hello?'

Her voice wasn't as Benedikt had ever heard it. He was used to clipped words and a shadow of suspicion. But her voice was mellow, with a warm, husky edge that made the flesh at his nape tighten and his groin stir.

He frowned. 'Annalena? Where are you?'

His staff had assured him she hadn't left her rooms, but he'd tried the landline several times already, finally resorting to her mobile phone.

'Where do you think, since you sent a stream of visitors to keep me out of mischief?'

She didn't sound quite so languid now, but there was still something about her tone…

'So you admit you're a mischief-maker?'

To his surprise that elicited a gurgle of laughter, rich and velvety. He shifted in his office chair on the far side of the palace, horrified at how her casual laugh went straight to his gonads.

'If only you knew. I was always the good girl. Serious, studious.'

Benedikt's imagination took the idea and ran with it.

Instead of a dirndl or jeans and T-shirt, his mind supplied a fitted pencil skirt, high-collared shirt and heels. Her green eyes surveyed him over clear glasses with an invitation at odds with her buttoned-up clothes. And she was pouting, her plush mouth pure invitation.

She looked like an incredibly alluring librarian. He could imagine her descending a tall library ladder, book in hand, the tight fit of her skirt lovingly outlining her backside and slender legs. His fingers twitched as if to reach for her.

Benedikt cleared his throat. Since when did he have librarian fantasies?

Not librarian fantasies. Fantasies about Annalena. Remember last night's dreams?

He adjusted his trousers where they'd grown tight.

She spoke again, saving him from the need to reply. 'My grandmother demanded good behaviour. I had to be a role model.'

Benedikt rubbed his jaw and sank back in his chair. 'I know how that feels.'

Even if he baulked at sharing real power, his father had been adamant Benedikt be the perfect crown prince because that reflected on him.

'You too? Did you ever rebel?'

'All the time. But not in public.'

From the moment he could choose for himself he'd spent most of his time outside Prinzenberg, returning only when necessary. It had made his father furious but he'd put up with it when he'd realised Benedikt's growing business acumen led to sizeable profits. Profits he'd hoped to redirect to his own coffers.

'And you? Were you serious and studious all the time?'

Her next breath held a hint of another chuckle and Benedikt felt his skin heat. 'I might, *occasionally*, have let my hair down.'

For a man who considered himself pragmatic and achievement-orientated his imagination was suddenly working overtime. Now it supplied a tantalising image of Annalena with her gleaming hair loose across her breasts. She leant back against heaped pillows, her only garment a lace negligée that revealed more than it concealed of her body. He was kneeling above her, lowering himself...

'How?' he croaked. 'How did you let your hair down?'

'The usual. Sneaking down to the local festival late at night, hanging out with other teenagers, tasting the local beer.'

'Just as well your grandmother didn't find out.'

She had the reputation of being a tartar.

'Oh, she knew. She told me later she was pleased to see I had the spirit and ingenuity to sneak out to be with my friends. She might be a stickler for duty and protocol but she's no snob. She believes in the value of individuals, no matter what their supposed social status.'

He digested that. There was more to the old lady than he'd thought. Just like her granddaughter.

'That's where our families differ. My father wanted me to spend my time only with *important* people. Ones who could be of value to him in future. He wasn't what you call a man of the people.'

Benedikt spun his office chair to face the window, taking in the nightscape of the capital's lights.

'That doesn't sound like much fun.'

He frowned. Was that a trace of pity he heard?

'Don't worry, you weren't the only one to sneak out and enjoy themselves.'

Though in his case he hadn't just sat around, drinking beer. He'd developed a taste for fast cars and hot women early. At one stage he'd also sought to deaden the emptiness of his personal life at the roulette wheel, before he realised how pointless that was. After that, and with his grandfather's encouragement, he'd sought his thrills in the business sphere and occasional rock climbing. As for women, he'd become much more discriminating, while avoiding serious relationships.

'Why did you call, Benedikt?'

'I thought we'd eat together. Discuss how you got on today. But I'm told you requested a meal on a tray. Are you all right?'

'Perfectly fine, thanks. But I want a quiet night. I assumed we'd talk tomorrow.'

He should be pleased. That gave him the evening free to work.

Strangely though, he felt…let down. Had he been looking forward to sharing a meal with her?

No, it was merely that he'd planned to discuss some of the many things they needed to cover before the coronation.

'You're exhausted from trying on dresses?'

He heard what sounded strangely like a splash then she spoke, not quite so relaxed now. 'You should try it some time. It takes *hours*. It's easier for men. Once they have your measurements, making formal clothes is pretty standard. But for women there are so many variables, not only colour and style but how you stand and carry yourself. And that's just one dress. Your Ms Becker said you'd given orders for a whole new wardrobe.'

Annalena's voice was suddenly razor-sharp.

Because he wanted her to look like a queen? What was wrong with that?

'It's necessary. From the night of the ball you'll be in the public eye. You'll need to look the part, not only when our engagement photos are taken and at the coronation.'

'I understand that and I've agreed on a dress for the ball and a couple of others. But I prefer not to use just one designer. I'll organise the rest myself, including the wedding dress.'

It was better to patronise a variety of makers yet Benedikt hesitated. Annalena had admitted she wasn't used to the royal court and what he'd seen of her wardrobe...

'My team can provide a list of designers. Your dress for the wedding and our coronation needs to be spectacular.'

He heard an impatient huff. 'Don't worry, I'm not going to sabotage the day by wearing something that lets us both down. I've already contacted a designer in Edelforst.'

Edelforst! The province was best known for agriculture and traditional handcrafts. It *was* beginning to make a name in medical research and robotics, but not, as far as he knew, women's fashion.

He had a momentary picture of her arriving at the grand cathedral in a dirndl and apron.

'I—'

'This isn't negotiable, Benedikt. If I have to go through with this marriage, I'll at least wear something designed and made in my home province.'

He pinched the bridge of his nose, trying to relinquish the need to keep control of every important detail.

Just because she chooses tradition and comfort over glamour it doesn't mean she doesn't know how to dress for the occasion.

This was a test. If they were going to marry, a level of trust was needed.

Unfortunate that the real legacy he'd got from his father was to trust sparingly. There'd been his mother and grandfather and now Matthias. He could count those he'd ever trusted completely on the fingers of one hand.

His father had mercilessly used any weakness to coerce others into doing his bidding, or to hurt them just because he could. No one had been spared, especially not his wife and son. Karl had only been interested in people for what he could take from them.

Annalena wasn't like that. Given the chance, she'd run from him and this marriage. Her honesty about that was strangely reassuring.

'As long as they can guarantee finishing in time.'

'Don't worry, the design's already sorted and she's calling in favours to get the hand-stitching done in time.'

Hand stitching. That sounded disturbingly amateur. But what did he know about dressmaking? All that mattered was that they married.

'Right.' He swivelled to face the desk and the work waiting for him. 'I'm glad you're okay. But we've got a lot to discuss. I'll meet you at eight tomorrow in my office.'

'I'll be there. I—' There was a clatter as if she'd dropped the phone.

'Annalena?'

'Sorry, I was reaching for my glass of wine and almost dropped the phone in the bath.'

She was drinking wine in the bath while he was sitting here facing a load of paperwork? Negotiating over her official wardrobe while lolling, naked…?

'Benedikt? Are you there?'

He scrubbed a hand around his neck. 'Yes, still here. But I have to go. I'll see you at eight.'

He ended the call before she could say more. What she'd already said was enough.

A ragged laugh escaped.

The woman had surely been sent to test his limits, as a king and an all too fallible man.

Forget librarian fantasies. In the far wing of the palace, Annalena reclined in a bath, naked, drinking wine. He could be there in minutes. He *wanted* to be there.

Except when they became intimate it would be on *his* terms, after they'd signed a marriage contract. After he'd got what he wanted: both the throne and therefore the country safe.

He gritted his teeth, opening the detailed reports on the dam. The print blurred because his unruly imagination kept relaying images of a naked, glistening Annalena.

It was going to be a long, hard evening.

CHAPTER NINE

THREE DAYS LATER Annalena stood in Benedikt's study. The room with its full bookshelves and comfortable leather chesterfields felt familiar, almost cosy, since she'd spent so much time here.

There'd been so many details to discuss and agree on. But today was different. It wasn't just the pair of them.

Apart from Benedikt's assistant, Matthias, there were half a dozen witnesses to today's formalities. All male, all holding important government positions, and all serious, their expressions ranging from sombre to aghast, making her feel more than ever like an unwelcome outsider.

Annalena kept her expression serene despite the crash of her heart against her ribs.

Benedikt sat at the desk, signing document after document with a confident flourish.

With their dark suits and long faces, the men gave a funereal air to the proceedings.

Annalena's green and silver dirndl seemed festive, almost frivolous by comparison. But her new wardrobe wasn't ready and these were the only formal clothes she'd brought.

How would these disapproving men have looked if she'd appeared in jeans and a T-shirt, the ones she wore for exploring the vast palace grounds? Her lips twitched and she looked up to see Matthias nod genially in her direction.

That tiny show of solidarity warmed her. She'd tried not to dwell on negative thoughts but felt very much alone.

Half an hour ago Benedikt had told her she was doing the right thing. But it was hard to believe, now their agreement was about to become real.

He put his pen down and stood, his gaze catching hers.

More warmth, a sizzle that flooded her body and made her pulse beat hard and low, but Annalena didn't trust it. He made her feel things she shouldn't. How could she believe his reassurances?

You have no other option.

She was in a corner with no escape.

Squaring her shoulders, she walked to the desk and sat. The royal desk, a huge antique used by generations of kings. Now here she was, an interloper.

She might have a right to sit here because of the blood that flowed in her veins, but it felt wrong. Obviously those around her felt the same. Her life was supposed to be elsewhere. She had a career, friends—

Benedikt's strong hand appeared before her, holding a gold fountain pen. 'When you're ready, Annalena.'

He stood close but didn't crowd her. She had a momentary flash of surprise, registering that she'd grown accustomed to him being near. Her body still reacted with regrettable predictability when he got close, but he didn't intimidate her. It was the disapproving old men glowering from the far side of the desk who did that.

She took the pen, straightened her shoulders and smiled coolly at her audience, refusing to let them see she was rattled. A couple of nervous smiles met hers.

Perhaps they weren't all disapproving, just concerned.

Who could blame them? She wasn't cut out for this, knew nothing about ruling the country.

Focus on the positive. You're a quick learner. You have some skills and people you can consult when in doubt.

Suppressing a sigh, she looked at the papers before her. In a gesture of good faith, Benedikt had signed first, ending the dam project, then signing the marriage contract and the documents giving her the right to rule jointly with him.

Even so, she read every word, ignoring the restless shuffle of feet. Finally, when she managed to steady her hand, she began to sign.

The final document was the marriage agreement.

Annalena flexed her fingers. They were stiff as if she'd been writing all morning. The words blurred, formal clauses turning into gobbledygook.

She blinked, trying to clear her vision.

She wasn't a romantic, but she'd assumed one day she'd marry for love. Or at least marry someone she liked.

Did she like Benedikt?

Sometimes she liked him too much. There were times when it felt as if they hovered on the brink of something more than reluctant acceptance.

Don't you want more than acceptance? Don't you want to be valued for yourself? Not for your claim to the throne?

Annalena swallowed over the constriction in her throat. She didn't have that luxury. Yet this felt wrong, promising to share her life, *herself* with a man she barely knew.

Someone on the other side of the desk coughed but beside her Benedikt stood steady, unmoving. As usual, she felt his presence without even turning her head.

Repressing a sigh, she grabbed the pen and signed.

There was no going back. She only hoped she hadn't just made the biggest mistake of her life.

* * *

'Don't leave, Annalena.'

She cast a longing look at the door closing behind the departing men. Now it was done, she needed time to gather her thoughts and her shaky equilibrium.

Because no matter what duty decreed, it was tough knowing her life would never be the same.

An hour in the woodland beyond the formal gardens would restore her calm. Being outside in the natural world had always been her go to when things got tough.

Was it any wonder she'd become a botanist?

'I have phone calls to make.'

She'd promised to phone her grandmother after the contract was signed. She turned to find Benedikt watching her, head tilted as if the better to scrutinise her.

The man who was going to be her husband.

Adrenaline shot through her bloodstream.

'I won't keep you long.'

'Of course.' She stifled an unfamiliar sensation that felt too much like panic and made herself walk back to the desk where he stood.

'It will be okay, Annalena, as long as we work together.'

His words and the expression in his eyes surprised her. She'd spent the days resenting the situation she found herself in. Yet he wasn't an ogre, just, she hoped, a man trying to do right by his country.

Had he read her fear? The idea was insupportable. She didn't want his pity. She'd spent her life standing up for herself and her people. Now she needed to be his equal if she were to have any chance of making this relationship work. A lifetime's lessons from her redoubtable Oma came to her aid as she wiped the frown from her face, offering him an expression of calm certainty.

'Yes, that's the only way. What did you want to discuss?'

For a second longer his gaze held hers then he looked down to something in his hand. 'We'll announce our betrothal at the ball in a couple of days. Plus there's a session booked for official photos. You'll need this.'

He held his hand out to reveal a green velvet box. A ring box.

'Oh.'

Her heart pounded so high it felt as if it tried to escape via her throat. Her cheeks flushed on a rush of heat before the ice forming in the pit of her stomach counteracted it.

He pressed a button and the lid popped to reveal a dazzling ring. It was plain but for the large, emerald-cut stone of clear, deep green that shone with inner fire.

Her grandmother owned a substantial jewellery collection but Annalena had never seen any piece so beautiful.

'It's from the treasury. You're welcome to choose something else if you prefer, but I thought this suited you.'

She raised her eyes. 'Oh?'

'The colour matches your eyes. And—' he lifted his shoulders '—because of its simplicity.'

Everything inside stilled. 'Because I'm simple?'

The last few days, with endless sessions about royal responsibilities and protocol, had left her fully aware of her ignorance in such matters, feeling more than ever out of her depth. But she'd thought she'd learned well.

She and Benedikt had been at loggerheads from the first but he'd never offered insults.

'Of course not!' Lines carved across his forehead. 'If anything, you're complex and not to be underestimated.' He paused. 'I was referring to your beauty. It's unfussy and natural. The ring reminded me of that.'

Annalena had no words. He thought her complex and

not to be underestimated? That made her sound like a worthy opponent.

But beautiful? She had even features and her eyes were an unusually pure green. Did he think she needed flattery? Did unfussy and natural mean unsophisticated? But her self-esteem didn't hinge on what he thought.

He probably felt it necessary to say *something* complimentary when presenting an engagement ring. Words of affection, much less love, would be insulting.

Yet she couldn't banish the tiny curl of delight deep inside at the compliment. Remarkably he'd made her feel special. Not what she envisaged from the man forcing her hand.

'Thank you, Benedikt. It's good you thought of a ring. I'd completely forgotten. It would have looked odd if I'd appeared without the appropriate prop.'

She took it out and slipped it on. It was a little snug, making her hyperconscious of its weight around her finger. Or perhaps that was because she didn't usually wear rings.

She moved her hand, transfixed by the gorgeous ring. An emerald? Probably, since it came from the treasury.

Annalena forced a smile to her lips. 'It looks regal, doesn't it? Perfect for the part I'm playing.'

Benedikt strode the long corridor to the guest wing. They were due to open the ball soon, but first he needed to see Annalena in her suite.

In case she's a no-show?

No, she'd given her word.

Because you want to vet what she's wearing? You don't trust her fashion sense?

That was the least of his worries. The designer knew what was needed. Annalena's outfit for the engagement photos couldn't have been better. The tailored skirt and jacket in a deep rose colour had been a perfect foil for her colouring. She'd looked elegant and attractive.

Yet her smiles hadn't reached her eyes and she'd been as wooden as a marionette when the photographer asked them to stand together. It had been hard finding convincing photos to project the image of an eager bride and groom.

She hadn't deliberately tried to sabotage the shoot, but her discomfort had been clear.

His jaw clenched. Photos could be airbrushed but tonight they'd be on show before hundreds of curious spectators. When he announced their engagement everyone needed to be convinced it was real. That it was what they both wanted.

What he *didn't* need was a bride-to-be who looked as if she were stepping onto a hangman's scaffold. Or one who regarded the flawless emerald on her ring finger as a *prop*.

How mistaken he'd been, thinking she'd like the ring. As soon as he'd seen it he'd wanted to see it on her finger. Almost as if he wanted to mark her as his own. It was a primitive, possessive instinct that didn't match their situation at all and made him uncomfortable whenever he thought of it.

Her response had drained his satisfaction at finding the perfect piece.

Stupid to feel rebuffed over a piece of jewellery. There were more important things at stake. Like making tonight look convincing.

Women had always been easy for him. He was used to their interest, their attention, their desire. He'd never imagined he'd have to coach a woman into acting as if she wanted to be with him.

He reached her suite, knocked and entered at the sound of her voice.

Midstride over the threshold, he halted. His hand clenched on the doorknob, his bow tie seemed to tighten around his throat. There was a thrumming in his ears as she moved towards him. He tried to swallow but it felt ridiculously difficult, as if he'd forgotten how.

All that in just a second. Then he stepped forward, closing the door behind him.

'Annalena, you look spectacular.' So spectacular, his voice sounded as if he spoke over ground glass.

He'd come intending to compliment her, to put her at ease before tonight's function. But this was no compliment, just a statement of fact.

She wore her hair up, not in an old-fashioned plaited coronet, but a sleek twist. Her face was different, her eyes smokier, her cheekbones accentuated and her mouth…

Her mouth.

He made himself drag his gaze away.

Her dress was simple yet stunning. Strapless, it was shaped to skim her body, glorying in her curves before falling in a straight column to the floor. There were no puffy skirts or outlandish ornamentation. Just Annalena, classically sophisticated and heartbreakingly beautiful.

The dress was emerald green like her eyes. The neckline dipped a little between her breasts, edged with what looked like diamonds.

She wore no jewellery except her ring, but from her shoulders, attached to the dress, hung a transparent, full-length cape of green studded with a galaxy of diamonds.

Benedikt hauled in air to constricted lungs.

'Thank you.' Her voice had a husky edge he liked. 'So do you. Formal evening clothes suit you.'

He shook his head. There was no comparison. He moved closer, something inside him dipping as she stiffened.

That wouldn't do, not tonight.

His concern wasn't just for the image they'd project. He hated her instinctive withdrawal.

Deliberately he conjured a light tone as he stopped before her. 'They look like tiny stars. Did you raid the treasury for diamonds?'

Her eyes widened and she looked down at the filmy material cascading from her shoulders. Her hand lifted as if to touch, then fell. 'Just diamantés, not the real thing. Don't worry. The royal coffers are safe.'

A tiny smile curved her lips and lit her face.

If only he could entice that smile more often. Get her to smile that way at *him*. At this rate no one would be convinced by their betrothal announcement.

He dragged in much-needed oxygen and with it came an elusive scent. The light but seductive perfume of mountain meadows and spring flowers.

Warmth enveloped him like Alpine sunshine and he leaned in. Instantly she took a half-step back, making him clamp his jaw.

'You're early. We're not due to open the ball for a while.'

'Yet you're ready.'

She lifted her shoulders in a shrug that should have been casual but seemed jerky. 'I didn't want to run late. I wanted to look…right.'

It was the first time she'd come close to admitting to nerves or uncertainty. As if to make up for it, she held her head high, her expression calm.

Benedikt wasn't fooled. He felt her tension. 'You look amazing. You'd be the belle of the ball even without our announcement.'

Her expression was quizzical. 'Thank you. Let's hope it goes smoothly.'

'That's why I'm here. There's something we need to fix before we appear in public.'

She frowned. 'Fix? All the arrangements are made. Your staff have been force-feeding me information on the guests for days, not to mention details of how the evening will proceed and every possible etiquette issue.'

'You'll deal with all that easily. And I'll be with you if you're unsure about anything.'

'So what's the problem?'

'This.'

He reached out and touched her hand. Immediately she flinched before standing stiffly, as unresponsive as a piece of wood.

'Are you scared of me?'

'Of course I'm not scared.'

Predictably her chin lifted. But her poise was undercut by the way she clamped her teeth into her bottom lip. He wanted to soothe the soft flesh with his own.

'Do you find me abhorrent?' He didn't believe it but had to ask. 'Every time we come close you stiffen up. At the photo shoot you looked like you wanted to be anywhere else but with me.'

'What do you want me to say, Benedikt? I didn't ask for this.' She waved her hand in a gesture that encompassed both him and the palace. 'You know I don't want it.'

He'd had a long, difficult week too, as difficult as hers. His patience snapped.

'You think I wanted things to work out this way?' He'd never wanted to marry. He'd seen close up how poisonous and destructive marriage could be. Only his sense of duty forced his hand, and the hope he'd do better than his parents. 'This is bigger than you or me. Bigger than our personal wants. We agreed that.'

Her head tipped back, making him realise he'd stepped in close. But she didn't look intimidated. Her hands were on her hips, her eyebrows arching superciliously. She'd never looked more desirable.

Light flashed off her emerald ring as she gesticulated. 'Which is why I'm dressed like this, ready to go through with tonight's farce. I'm delivering on my side of the deal.'

Her eyes glittered, diffidence replaced by pride and a challenge he felt deep in his gut.

Now this wasn't about a show for the world to see. It was about him and her.

He wanted to curl his arm around her back, tug her close and feel those soft curves against his hardness. He wanted her eyes to turn brilliant with sensual invitation and later, with sated delight.

He wanted Annalena. And despite her anger now, he'd seen the looks she'd sent him this last week when she thought he wasn't paying attention. Looks that made him suspect her tension wasn't about repugnance but something quite different.

Benedikt forced his hands to stay at his sides rather than reach for her.

'It's not enough. You need to do more.'

'More? I'm *marrying* you. There *is* no more.'

He was already shaking his head. 'It's not enough to go through the motions. You have to make it look convincing. If you flinch every time I get near, no one will believe in our marriage or our partnership as rulers.'

Her eyes darkened and for a second he wondered if he read fear in her eyes. Then the illusion disintegrated. He saw only impatience.

'You want me to nestle close and simper?'

A bark of laughter escaped. 'I can't imagine you simpering but I'd love to see you try.'

He'd enjoy her nestling close, reaching for him.

Slowly her mouth curled into a rueful smile. 'You're right, I wouldn't have a clue how.'

Benedikt waited. Now her flash of anger had disintegrated, she seemed to mull over his words.

'I'm not a good actor.'

'Of course you are. Remember the day you strode into my office and threatened to take the crown from me? You were so self-assured, as if you had no doubts that you'd succeed. But you can't have known for sure it would work.'

'Anger can make anyone brave.'

'Maybe. But what about when we signed the marriage agreement? The witnesses commented later on your poise. You took it all in your stride with complete confidence.' Benedikt lowered his voice. 'But I saw how your hand shook and how you needed time to bring yourself to sign.'

She chewed her lip. 'You weren't supposed to notice.'

But he had and his admiration for her had soared.

'Think of all those times when you've had to project the image people expect, as Princess of Edelforst, or presenting at some academic conference. You're good at hiding trepidation, good at being the person people need you to be.'

Her eyes were wide and her lips parted as if he'd shocked her to the core.

'Did you really think I was so oblivious I wouldn't notice? You play a good game, Annalena, but don't forget I grew up learning those same skills. I can hide my feelings and put on a public face too.'

She breathed deeply, her sigh fluttering across his chin. 'This isn't quite the same.'

He didn't have a name for the emotion that rippled across

her features, but it made him regret that he'd had to force her hand.

'No. Not for either of us.'

Though he had no qualms about touching her. Increasingly it seemed the most natural thing in the world.

Warmth closed around his hand and he looked down to see slim fingers curling around his. His heart lurched. It felt like a breakthrough. Instantly he was reminded of those breathless moments in the summerhouse when he'd caressed her and been so sure she wanted him.

'Is that better?'

He looked up to find his gaze snared by gorgeous green eyes. 'It's a start.'

A hint of a frown skated over her forehead. 'What more do you want? We're standing close and I'm touching you.'

'But what if I reach for you? Will you startle and pull away before you have a chance to school your features?'

Her mouth crimped at the corners. 'I'll work on it, okay? Maybe you could warn me if you're going to touch me.'

'And how would that play out in public?' He shook his head. 'That won't always be possible.'

'Okay, okay.' She blew out a gusty breath. 'I take your point. I promise not to tense up if you touch me.'

'Easily said, Annalena.'

Her eyes narrowed. 'You don't trust me?'

He shrugged, enjoying the spark in her eyes. Seeing her feisty and fearless did something to him, his libido especially.

'It's not a matter of trust, but getting acclimatised to my touch. But we don't have time to take things slowly. How about we take a short cut?'

She tilted her head, scrutinising him like some scientific specimen. Did she even notice that he'd turned his hand to thread his fingers through hers?

'What sort of short cut?'

Benedikt failed to repress his smile. 'A kiss. Then you'll see you've nothing to fear from me. After that having me touch your back or your arm will be a walk in the park. What do you say? Shall we?'

CHAPTER TEN

WHAT SHE SHOULD say was a resounding *'No'*. Especially when he looked at her with that gleam in his eyes. He didn't look like a man worried about public opinion. He *looked* like a man who wanted…her.

That stopped her throat and quickened her pulse. He was dangerous. But in that heady moment she welcomed his attention.

Was she projecting her own desire? He had few scruples about doing whatever it took to secure the throne and the country. Appearing interested in her was part of the deal. She'd be crazy to believe it was more than a calculated act.

But he had a point. What if she jumped at his touch in public? This marriage would elicit enough consternation without that.

Maybe a kiss would work as exposure therapy.

Maybe she'd grow blasé about his touch.

Maybe you want to find out what kissing Benedikt is like.

'One kiss.'

Where had that come from? She hadn't planned the words.

Annalena watched a smile unfurl across his face. She read approval but more too. Something that made her wonder if this was a good idea. But she couldn't back out. Showing fear was always a mistake.

Determined to get it over before she could think too much, she stepped so close their bodies almost touched.

She felt his body heat down her whole length. Except it was more than heat. It felt like thousands of sparks igniting across her skin.

All the more reason not to linger. Planting one hand on his chest, she tilted her head.

But her intention to press a brief kiss to his lips died as she registered the thud of his heart beneath his jacket. Watched his eyes zero in on her lips.

Her breath escaped in a sigh because she *felt* that look like a caress. Her pulse hammered and her chest shuddered as she sucked in air.

Just get it done. A few seconds and it will be over.

She rose to brush her mouth against his.

Annalena blinked, stunned to discover his lips were soft. Even that cursory touch brought with it a taste of... She couldn't name the flavour except she liked it.

Benedikt didn't respond, didn't move, his gaze focused on her mouth in a way that made her imagine her lips throbbed. They parted and she licked them, trying to draw in more of that taste. *His* taste.

A fiery arc of heat shot down her body, past her nipples and stomach to the hollow between her thighs.

Golden-brown eyes met hers and one slashing dark eyebrow lifted as if to say *Is that the best you can do?*

He was right. That wasn't a kiss. Yet she was torn between competing instincts. To be cautious and step away. Or be bold and fit her mouth to his.

In the end it was a mix of determination not to be seen as weak and the lure of irresistible temptation.

She put her other hand on his shoulder, holding herself steady as she rose and covered his mouth with hers.

He didn't move but that didn't matter because she knew exactly what she wanted. Tilting her head, she closed her eyes and moved her lips, brushing, nibbling, tasting. The rich, unique taste of him was addictive and she wanted more.

Her fingers drifted up to cup the hot flesh of his neck, thumb on his jaw and fingertips buried in his short hair.

Finally he moved, angling his head to give better access.

Her breath stalled as delight punched hard. She wanted...

Too much. Far more than this tentative caress, yet still Benedikt didn't reciprocate. Did he feel nothing? Not the tiniest spark of pleasure? Was this truly just about her acclimatising to his presence?

Hurt pride seared.

Maybe, like some of his staff, he found her unsophisticated. She'd heard a stifled giggle in the royal offices the other day. From the corner of her eye she'd seen Ida Becker whispering to another woman and caught the words '...wearing a dirndl like a milkmaid.'

As if their national dress were embarrassing!

As if *Annalena* had anything to be ashamed of because she tried to deal with people honestly, not playing at one-upmanship.

Annalena didn't stop to ponder why that provoked her. Why Benedikt's unresponsiveness became unbearable. She simply followed her instinct, stroking her tongue between his lips, demanding entry, then following that delicious taste and exploring the lush mystery of his mouth.

She clasped his head with both hands, tentative no longer as she delved deep and discovered...

Oh.

A shudder raced from her head to her soles as his tongue slid against hers, curling and drawing her deep into plush, velvety warmth that was more inviting than any place she'd ever been.

Something jolted through her like an electric shock. Every sense deepened. Colours appeared in the darkness behind her eyes like a kaleidoscope reflecting sunlight. The scent and taste of him deepened. The satin of his skin beneath her palms and the thick silk of his hair against her fingertips made her hands curl possessively. She *heard* the twin thrum of their pulses, beating in sync.

She'd kissed before. But the last time had been a long time ago. How could she have forgotten?

Unless it hadn't been like this.

Disquiet filtered into her brain. Did he sense it? A second later it vanished as he roped his arms around her, tugging her flush against his body.

Annalena gasped at the myriad sensations. All that hard, masculine heat. The heavy cushion of muscled thighs and broad chest. The slow track of one large hand settling low on her back and drawing her in. Benedikt's mouth moving with hers, his tongue coaxing and enticing.

Goosebumps broke out across her skin as he came alive against her, turning her foray into a mutual caress, deep and slow.

It felt as easy as if they'd done this a million times before. As inevitable as the sun rising over the Alps.

But more exciting than anything she knew.

Annalena stretched high, revelling in his solidity against her yearning body, the strength of long arms encircling her, pulling her close.

There was a muffled sound, a low hum, almost a growl, that she tasted in the back of her throat, and easy familiarity turned urgent. He led her deeper, into places she hadn't gone and she followed eagerly, utterly entranced.

She clung, grasping for purchase as her knees loosened and only his embrace kept her upright. Her blood effervesced like champagne and her toes curled as ribbons of delight danced through her.

Benedikt supported the back of her head in one hand as he bent low, taking her mouth with devastating thoroughness. Making her nipples pucker and her brain atrophy.

Deep within she felt a hungry twist of need. A hollow throb that began in her pelvis but resonated everywhere. Moisture dampened her new silk undies as arousal stirred.

The truth slammed into her brain. This kiss had nothing to do with hurt pride or proving a point, but everything to do with her response to Benedikt.

Annalena's hands tightened on his skull as she tried to climb his body, curving her spine to align her pelvis with his.

She tasted another low, masculine growl that sent her libido into overdrive.

Then, abruptly, nothing.

She heard breathing, harsh and uneven, gulped lungfuls of cold air and felt strong hands at her elbows. They held her as she wobbled on high heels, legs like overcooked spaghetti. Her hands clenched and opened, empty.

Stunned, she lifted impossibly heavy eyelids.

Benedikt loomed over her, dishevelled, lipstick-smeared and distant. His jaw was set, the mouth that had kissed her so voraciously a flat line.

Annalena blinked, barely taking in his rumpled hair and bow tie hanging loose, trying to read his searing gaze. She saw heat but was it from arousal or something else?

His gaze roved her face and her lips throbbed and parted. A second later he withdrew totally, stepping back and putting a world of space between them.

Well, that went well. You came undone while he...

She didn't want to think about how he felt. She had a horrible feeling that passionate kiss had been an experiment on his part, the passion all hers.

Annalena watched him roll his shoulders and straighten to his full height. He wasn't even out of breath whereas her heart hammered as she struggled to draw in oxygen, making her breasts rise and fall quickly.

That's the least of your worries. Never show weakness to an enemy, remember?

Except he hadn't felt like an enemy.

'Was that enthusiastic enough?' she murmured, hiding a wince at her husky, broken voice. 'Not that we'll have to go that far to convince our guests.'

His eyes narrowed and she'd swear she saw annoyance flicker across his set features.

'You're saying that was an act?'

Benedikt's tone was clipped. She hated the contrast, hated herself for what she'd done. How could she let him affect her that way?

She shrugged and walked past him, grateful for the sheer determination that kept her steady on high heels despite feeling as if her bones had melted. 'It wasn't…unpleasant and I wanted to be thorough. Isn't that how exposure therapy works?'

She didn't want to see his reaction to her lie. But she'd tramp over hot coals rather than admit she'd lost her senses as soon as he'd kissed her back.

A shiver ran through her. Their upcoming marriage was more daunting now than ever. She'd just proved she wanted her husband-to-be. But he'd pulled back from her. He might simulate passion but that was all it was, a sham.

Hurt welled. An echo of the ancient self-pity she'd thought she'd conquered years ago. At never wholly fitting in. At always being different. The orphan brought up by an old lady regarded locally with mixed awe, reverence and trepidation. The girl from the castle, privileged but hemmed in by duty and expectation.

Annalena stopped at a mirror over the fireplace to gather her tattered control. She was a mess. Lipstick gone, hair coming down and a flush of sexual arousal emblazoned her throat and cheeks. Even her eyes looked different, heavy-lidded as if she'd just woken. Or left a lover's bed.

'It wasn't *unpleasant*?'

His voice was edged like a sharpened blade. She should have known he'd take her words as a challenge. She *had* known, and struck out rather than admit he'd affected her. But she didn't have the energy to deal with his ego. Not when her world was crumbling.

It had just been a kiss yet it felt like far more. Shockwaves reverberated through her and she wanted to curl up, alone in her room. Better yet, leave this place and never face him again.

A huff of laughter escaped as she tidied her hair. No chance of that!

'You find this funny, Annalena?'

In the mirror she saw he'd moved to stand behind her, tall, broad-shouldered and compelling. Something turned over in her belly and her pelvic muscles pulled tight.

You really are in trouble.

He could use her susceptibility against her. She had to defend against that.

'Not at all.' Defiantly she met his stare in the glass. 'I was thinking how much I'd give to be anywhere else.'

His expression shifted and she almost fancied she saw understanding in his eyes. 'It will get easier, Annalena. I'm not your enemy.'

She wished she could believe it.

You have to believe it or this marriage will destroy you.

Was it possible their relationship might be like Oma's marriage? Not that there'd be love, she wasn't naive. But was friendship possible, or at least respect and cooperation?

Benedikt held her gaze. 'Whatever you're thinking, Annalena, this isn't the end of the world. It will be tough but we'll find a way.'

She pivoted and he was closer than she'd anticipated. So close her unrepentant heart thrummed in excitement. So much for gathering her tattered self-possession! Yet there was no glint of smugness in his eyes. Nothing but calm certainty.

Despite the gnawing hurt that he hadn't shared her desperate yearning, his expression settled a little of her tension. 'We'll be partners, Annalena. Is that so bad?'

Strange how the idea drew her. For so long she'd strived alone, fighting her battles with only her beloved Oma in the background, urging her on. Day to day Annalena had only herself. The thought of a partner, even if just for her formal responsibilities, was strangely attractive.

If she could set aside her doubts and trust him.

'Help me?' He took a handkerchief from his pocket and held it out.

After a moment Annalena took it, avoiding his fingers. She held the fabric that bore the warmth of his body. Then stepped close and raised the fine cotton to the lipstick smudge beside his mouth.

Again his scent engulfed her, making her insides squirm in excitement. But she concentrated on the stain, trying not to think of how it got there. Refusing to notice how his lips looked fuller from their kiss, or the quick pulse throbbing at his jaw.

When she stepped back it was to discover he'd retied his

bow tie. Of course he could do it perfectly without a mirror! She held out his handkerchief.

Benedikt retrieved it without brushing her fingers.

She was grateful, not disturbed that he understood her need for distance. But her movements were abrupt as she stepped away.

'I'll just be a moment.'

Annalena could have finished tidying her hair where she was. Her purse with her lipstick was nearby. But she needed more, needed something to shore up her courage.

Thirty seconds later she was in the bathroom, reaching for the other lipstick the make-up expert had suggested for tonight. A deep scarlet rather than the pink she'd initially worn, it smoothed across her swollen lips, creamy and soothing. The colour was darker and defiant.

No, she amended, not defiant. Assured. She looked like a confident woman unfazed by the stunning couture gown, the imposing man who'd be her companion or the pomp and glitter of a royal celebration. A woman at home among hordes of people who'd wonder if she had what it took to be Queen.

Fake it till you make it.

She grimaced at her reflection, then thought of the Grand Duchess of Edelforst who for thirty years had protected Annalena's true identity and safety, while single-handedly ensuring their homeland wasn't eviscerated by King Karl and his greedy cohort.

It's your turn to step up, Annalena. No going back.

The grand ballroom had never looked more stupendous.

Rows of antique chandeliers glittered brilliantly after staff had spent a week polishing every crystal facet. Enormous mirrors lined the walls, reflecting an infinity of light and the shifting colours of the formally dressed crowd. On one side, French doors stood open to a terrace with views over the gardens where fountains played and spotlights turned night into day.

Everybody who was anybody in Prinzenberg, and for that matter Europe, was here.

And none, Benedikt realised as he escorted Annalena down the length of the room, outshone the woman beside him.

She took his breath away. Still.

The way she'd looked when he'd entered her room, soignée and alluring. But that was only part of it. The way she *tasted*. He'd kissed many women but none tasted like her. Delicious. Intriguing. *Addictive*.

When she'd clutched him, leaning up to take what she wanted, he'd rejoiced. Not because of how they'd look together at the ball, but because finally he had the real Annalena without artifice or caution.

It had been like holding a goddess in his arms, seductive and awe-inspiring, her passion so powerful it called to him at an elemental level.

What had begun as an exercise to make their partnership look convincing had escalated into a lust-fuelled adventure.

His one saving grace was that he hadn't backed her onto a sofa and ravished her so thoroughly that neither of them would have been fit to attend the ball. She had no idea how close he'd come to lifting those silky skirts and having her there and then.

He could have because, despite her horrified reaction later, she'd been as swept away as he.

When he'd forced himself away and seen her, eyes slumbrous with invitation, hair tumbling about her shoulders from his urgent grasping, lips dark and swollen… She'd tempt a saint, something Benedikt had never aspired to be.

His stride now was shorter than usual. Not only because of the need to acknowledge greetings and make introductions, but because walking in his semi-aroused state was uncomfortable.

He glanced at the woman beside him, so composed, wearing the hint of a smile. Any concerns she mightn't cope tonight disintegrated. She looked every inch the Queen she was about to become.

Except for that mouth. He swallowed, trying to ignore the increasing pressure in his groin. Those scarlet lips belonged to a seductress, not a monarch.

His gaze raked their audience and sure enough most of the men were gaping as if they'd never seen a woman before.

And she's all mine...or will be soon.

'Your Majesty.'

He paused, recognising Colonel Ditmar bowing before him.

'Colonel, I'm pleased you could be here.'

'Thank you.' The old man shifted his attention to Annalena. 'Princess, may I say you look ravishing?'

'You may, Colonel. I'll accept such flattery since you're an old friend.'

Ditmar protested there was no flattery and Annalena's smile grew wide. Benedikt was glad she had at least one friend here.

'Your Majesty.'

He turned and there was Countess Heldenbruck. Her black hair shone like a raven's wing, the deep blue of her dress highlighting her creamy complexion and dark eyes.

Regret slammed into Benedikt. Not because he couldn't marry her as he'd once considered, but because he'd have preferred to tell her of his impending wedding in private. That hadn't been an option. He couldn't have risked a leak of the news he'd announce tonight before everything was in place.

'Elise, it's good to see you. You're looking very fine.'

'So are you, Your Majesty.'

They exchanged light pleasantries, but he was acutely aware of her questioning stare, almost hidden by her smile. And how, after one quick glance at Annalena's ring finger, she hadn't looked that way again.

Suddenly his collar felt too snug. Was Annalena right? He and Elise had never discussed marriage or a relationship. But had he inadvertently raised expectations?

He'd been so determined to identify a suitable spouse who wouldn't demand too much, he hadn't considered her perspective.

His gut tightened. He'd told himself he never used people the way his father had. But the lines between them were more blurred than he'd thought. He'd been as ruthless as Karl, fixated only on getting what he wanted without considering others.

Too late to worry about your conscience. You're making Annalena marry you, even knowing she hates the idea.

'Elise, let me introduce you.' He turned to Annalena. 'Princess, I'd like to introduce Countess Heldenbruck. Countess, I don't believe you know Princess Annalena of Edelforst.'

After greetings were exchanged, Annalena surprised him by saying, 'I believe I know your cousin Paul, Countess.'

'Really?' Elise's smile looked less brittle than a moment ago. 'He hasn't lived in Prinzenberg for years.'

'I met him on a field trip in Scandinavia.' She continued with an amusing anecdote about a research trip that involved dog sledding into the wilderness. She painted Elise's cousin as a saviour when the team ran into difficulties. Benedikt watched with gratitude as the Countess's expression eased.

A few minutes later they moved through the press of guests towards a dais. The buzz of conversation grew loud with speculation. Some of those closest had noticed the emerald on Annalena's finger and hurried to spread the word.

But no one broached the subject with him. Protocol demanded a royal announcement.

Between nods and smiles Annalena murmured, 'That was her? The woman you mentioned?'

Benedikt's pace faltered, his head snapping round. But Annalena's expression revealed only the same mild pleasure she'd shown since entering the room.

She was even more perspicacious than he'd thought. Neither he nor Elise had uttered anything but social niceties.

He should feel embarrassed, introducing his fiancée to the woman he'd considered marrying. But he'd planned a convenient marriage, not a love match. Annalena could hardly be jealous.

'It was.'

'She's extremely beautiful, and, I think, intelligent.'

She was right. Benedikt wouldn't accept any less in a wife, but he couldn't say that to the woman he was forcing into marriage.

'Yes, she is.'

But no more than you.

Something else he couldn't say.

'Thanks for putting her at ease. I hadn't realised…' He shook his head. 'I put her in a difficult position. It was cruel of me not to warn her about tonight.'

To his surprise Annalena's expression softened. 'I don't see how you could. There was too much at stake. But I'm glad you realise it.'

At the end of the room he slowed his step, holding her gaze. 'Ready?'

She nodded, making the crystals on her translucent cape shiver like winking stars. Her eyes were just as bright. He wished he knew what she was thinking.

Taking her hand, he guided her up the steps. The room hushed as they turned to face their audience.

He could have heard a pin drop when he made the announcements. First he introduced Annalena then explained they planned to marry and rule jointly.

Stunned silence spun out until someone nearby broke into cheers that were rapidly taken up until the ballroom swelled with the din.

There was no way of knowing how genuine the applause was. He saw stunned expressions, one or two heads shaking. But there were plenty of smiles too.

Meeting Annalena's eyes, he saw a flash of something he couldn't name. His conscience wavered and he realised with devastating clarity how much he asked of this woman. But he couldn't pull back.

'Shall we?'

He led her onto the dance floor. The crowd parted and the musicians struck up 'The Emperor Waltz'.

Annalena's fingers spasmed in his and he paused mid-step but she seemed to gather herself. 'Let's do this,' she whispered.

They paced to the centre of the enormous room and as the music swelled, he slipped his arm around her waist and drew her into a slow-turning circle.

She was posture perfect, breathtaking under the blaze of lights, and their steps matched as if they'd danced together for years.

Benedikt pulled her closer for their sedate duty waltz

under curious eyes. But when the pace of the music accelerated the dance turned into something more. The swirling music beat in his blood. The feel of Annalena, supple yet strong in his embrace, ignited an excitement, a mix of satisfaction and hunger that had nothing to do with the crowd or the crown.

Mysterious green eyes held his. Her breasts rose quickly and her lips parted as they sped down the room. The audience was a glittering blur.

His vision telescoped to the woman he held, the sensuality of her body against his and the heady, possessive beat of his blood.

Soon, soon, soon.

Suddenly he couldn't wait for their wedding.

CHAPTER ELEVEN

THEY MARRIED A scant two weeks later.

Never had time rushed so quickly. Annalena had returned to Edelforst, seeking solace in familiar work and faces but didn't find it. As she delivered on research goals and finalised contract negotiations, her inbox filled with messages from the palace. Questions to be answered, decisions to be made, reams of material to digest.

Then there were the calls. To be fair, Benedikt rarely called during business hours, like her, busy with his work. But early in the morning and in the evening she'd hear his deep voice, sometimes scratchy with tiredness, and her senses did an unwanted little shimmy of anticipation.

Those calls catapulted her back to the ball. The whirl of them dancing in harmony as if they *were* the perfect couple they tried to appear.

To the kiss. The wretched kiss that had upended all her certainty about what she *didn't* want from Benedikt.

'Annalena?'

Colonel Ditmar stood beside her, imposing in dress uniform. His kindly eyes met hers.

'Sorry. I was...' What? Wishing herself anywhere but here? 'Gathering myself.'

A brisk wind caught them on the cathedral's porch, making her glad she had no veil and wore her hair up. She refused to appear veiled like some virgin, passed from one male protector to another.

Even if the virgin part was true. How was she meant to navigate this marriage when Benedikt undid her so easily? His impact on her *had* to be down to her inexperience. The alternative was untenable.

'It's a big thing you're doing, my dear, but you're up to it. You'll make a wonderful queen. Your grandmother is proud of you and your parents would have been too.'

The colonel's sincerity as much as his words cut through her jangling nerves. She felt a warm glow, even as her mouth wobbled and she blinked suddenly scratchy eyes.

The thought of her parents approving was surprisingly strengthening. As for Oma, how Annalena wished she could be here. But the old lady's agoraphobia made that impossible. Annalena knew how frustrated she was by it, and how she hid it behind a brisk manner. Even now she'd be watching the live broadcast.

The realisation made Annalena straighten and grip her bouquet tighter.

'Thank you, Colonel, that means a lot.'

She turned to her attendants, a colleague's twelve-year-old twins. Wearing coronets of wildflowers and pretty dresses of pale spring green, they twitched the hem of her dress. 'Ready, girls?'

They hurried into position, their eagerness a stark contrast to her feelings.

The colonel nodded to an attendant. A trumpet fanfare sounded then the resonant notes of the massive pipe organ. Music rolled through the doorway, grand and ebullient. Celebratory. Annalena refused to acknowledge her stomach's nauseating churn. Instead she lifted her chin and let the colonel lead her forward.

Shafts of sunlight, coloured by ancient stained-glass windows, lit the massive heraldic flags hanging high above the congregation. The cathedral was packed. She saw suits and traditional festive clothes, beaming smiles and stares. All those people and she probably only knew a dozen.

It was easier to look at the guests than the tall figure at the end of the aisle. Yet how could she *not* look?

It felt as though a taut, invisible cord stretched between her and the man waiting at the end of the long red carpet.

Despite her best efforts, her gaze lifted. His eyes were on her, even from this distance she felt the snap and sizzle of his stare. His face looked chiselled, proud and imposing. Her insides did that appalling dance of awareness and her mouth tightened.

Then she remembered the millions watching the televised ceremony and forced a smile.

He was so close now she saw the amber-gold glow of his eyes. But she couldn't read his expression, just that his focus was totally on her. Was that triumph she read? Satisfaction? It couldn't be eagerness except for what this marriage brought him—the crown.

There was no more time for thinking. Her attendants took the bouquet. The colonel squeezed her hand and placed it in Benedikt's.

A tumble of feelings rocked her. Emotions she didn't want to acknowledge. How could one man's touch be so different to another's?

The priest spoke her name and she snapped her head around. But all through the ceremony Annalena felt distanced from it, as if separated by a wall of glass. She was aware only of Benedikt's hand holding hers and the thrum of her heartbeat. And her stilted voice as she spoke her vows.

Until the moment when a pleased voice said, 'You may now kiss the bride.'

Inevitably her thoughts flew to the kiss that had left her limp with need. Heat flooded her cheeks as she turned to her husband.

Her husband!

She swallowed and tilted her chin, lifting her face.

An expression cut across his sculpted face, so quickly she almost missed it. Annoyance. A fleeting frown of annoyance!

What the hell did he have to be annoyed about?

Then warm lips covered hers. She inhaled sharply, drawing in the stunningly familiar scent-taste of him. His hand covered her cheek as he tilted his head, a gesture that to the onlookers would appear tender, even possessive. His mouth moved on hers and suddenly she felt—

'That's enough,' she whispered through stiff lips.

Benedikt paused, mouth still brushing hers, then slowly lifted his head as a roar of delight rose from the crowd.

He smiled down at her and she knew the world would see a fairy-tale prince besotted with his bride. Only she knew his smile didn't reach eyes that stayed serious and watchful.

'One ceremony down,' he murmured. 'Only the coronation to go.'

Hours later Annalena stood in the sitting room of the new suite she'd been allocated, adjoining Benedikt's. Her face ached from smiling and her feet felt hot from so many hours in heels.

She'd discarded her shoes by the door. She'd thought of running herself a bath since she'd sent away the maid who'd been eager to assist. She wasn't up to dealing with other people, however helpful. But instead of relaxing in warm water, she found herself at the window, still in her heavy, satin wedding dress, watching the fireworks explode over the city as Prinzenberg celebrated.

'I thought you might like some refreshment. You didn't eat at the reception.'

Annalena swung around in a swish of long skirts, one hand going to her throat. Across the room, in the doorway to his rooms, stood Benedikt.

He'd discarded his jacket and cufflinks and rolled his sleeves to the elbow, baring strong, tanned forearms. His bow tie hung loose and his formal shirt was undone at the throat.

His air of undiluted sexiness stopped her breath. He had a vitality that proclaimed him far more than an office-bound administrator. Annalena wondered what he did in his spare time.

It took a second to register the tray he carried.

'I didn't hear you knock.' Was her voice too high?

'No. You were oblivious. You're a fan of fireworks?'

He moved into the room and put the tray on a low table. She saw canapés and fruit, pastries and a wine bottle nestled in the silver cooler.

A tickle of something that might have been excitement stroked her backbone. That wouldn't do. She couldn't allow herself to be wined, dined and charmed. Not if she wanted to be his equal. Benedikt threatened her equilibrium in ways she'd never experienced. She couldn't trust the yearning he made her feel because she feared that would make her vulnerable. Emotions had made her mother vulnerable and destroyed her.

'It's been a long day. I'm sorry, I'm not in the mood for company.'

'And I'm in no mood to be ignored.' His tone was even

but his words made her head rock back in shock. 'Listen, Annalena.' He moved closer. 'We've embarked on something together. Something big. We need to share, not shut each other out.'

In other circumstances his words might have softened her. But she remembered, vividly, his expression in the cathedral. He'd barely hidden his distaste.

'I agree. We need to work as a team. But not now. I'm tired.'

For a long moment Benedikt said nothing, merely surveyed her, then slowly shook his head. 'No, you're not. You're wired. I can see it from here, *feel* it. You're tense with excess energy.'

He was right. The adrenaline that had ridden her all day was still in her bloodstream. How did he know? It couldn't be that obvious.

'Okay, then. I'm not tired but I'd rather be alone.'

His gaze narrowed on hers and she felt like a specimen under a microscope. What did he see? The trouble was, the longer he stood there, so effortlessly charismatic, so annoyingly virile, the more her nerves jittered and her composure cracked.

Because for two weeks, underlying everything else she did had run the desire for *more* from Benedikt. More than that ravishing kiss. Though she knew it would leave her wide open in a way she couldn't afford. Though she now had confirmation that he really wasn't into her.

'If you feel that way I'll leave. But first tell me what's wrong. There's something, isn't there?'

A ragged laugh escaped. 'Apart from being blackmailed into marriage?'

Benedikt said nothing, merely waited, leaving her with the

disturbing feeling that she was overly emotional. She folded her arms across her waist, palms flat against heavy satin.

'You come to my room as if we're friends or lovers.' She licked dry lips. 'You talk about sharing, but I know what I saw in the cathedral. I'd rather you were honest about your feelings.'

His eyebrows scrunched down, furrows lining his brow. 'What did you see?'

Annalena gestured to his face. 'That. Your frown when you had to kiss me. Your feelings were obvious, to me at least.' She turned her palm towards him when he would have spoken. 'I don't mind that you don't *want* me in that way. But I'd rather you didn't lie and pretend we're anything more than partners in a cold-blooded, convenient match.'

She hurried on, gesturing to the tray he'd brought. 'I don't want champagne and midnight seduction, especially from a man who's not attracted to me. But give me time and I'm sure we can develop a good working relationship.'

'You read all that into a single frown?'

She shrugged. 'A frown you were quick to hide. I understand that. I know the kiss was just for show. But that expression was *real*.'

Benedikt moved closer, his face sombre. 'You're right. It was.'

Crazy how the confirmation felt like a punch to the chest. She felt winded, bracing her hands between the deep V of her neckline and her stomach. The sumptuous embroidery covering her bodice scratched her palms.

'I *wasn't* happy,' he went on with a bluntness that made her want to cringe. 'Because when you turned to me *your* expression gave you away. You held yourself like some stoic martyr, like a virgin about to be ravished. As if you couldn't bear my touch.'

Her breath hissed. Did he somehow know she was a virgin? Impossible.

'I thought we'd moved past that, Annalena. Our kiss the night of the ball proved that however much our actions are driven by duty, there's something personal here too.'

'All that kiss proved was that you're willing to use your… wiles to get what you want.'

One dark eyebrow shot high. 'Wiles?'

'You know what I mean. You're a good-looking man and know your way around women. That doesn't mean you were invested in the kiss, any more than I was.'

He studied her intently and a tide of heat rose over her breasts and throat.

'You're lying again. Just like you lied when you said you were tired.'

His words scratched her pride. Since when had she resorted to untruths? She'd been brought up to value honesty and honour.

Fury and frustration at herself bubbled so high it felt as though her skin was too tight to contain her feelings. She'd gone into this with her eyes open but tonight everything felt twisted and wrong. As if she were in danger of being overwhelmed.

'You want honesty? I honestly want you to leave this minute.'

'Because you think I don't want you.' Did the gold flecks in his eyes flare brighter? 'Because if I kiss you, you'll think I'm using *wiles*.'

Behind that serious expression he was laughing at her, she knew it. Annalena stalked across the space between them, getting in his face, releasing the pure blaze of anger that had burned for weeks.

'Don't mock me, Benedikt.'

She glared up at him, hating the sharp pang of appreciation at his sheer magnetism. Even now it tugged at something deep-seated and needy inside her.

His eyes danced and his mouth curved into a hard, tight smile that looked edgy and, if she didn't know better…ravenous. Instead of being cowed, she felt excitement stir. As if she welcomed the fact he wasn't so sanguine now.

'I wouldn't dare mock, Annalena. But you've accused me of lying and I can't let that stand.' He spread his hands, shoulders lifting. 'I can't convince you with words and I can't convince you with a kiss.'

His gaze zeroed in on her mouth and she had to resist the urgent need to moisten her lips.

'How can I show you that I want you, Annalena? Not just as a queen but a woman? Perhaps with this?'

Before she had time to register his intent, long fingers curled around her hand, pulling it down between them. Down to his groin.

He pressed her palm to the front of his dark trousers, against the long, rigid heat of an erection.

Annalena dragged in a stunned breath as her hand instinctively curled around him. Her grip firmed and she felt an answering throb.

Fascinated, she raised rounded eyes to his. 'Satisfied? That's one thing I can't feign. My *wiles* don't stretch that far.' That smile looked more like a grimace now. 'Just so we're absolutely clear, I want you. In my bed.'

Rocked to her core, she planted her other hand on his chest for balance, only to discover his heartbeat, pounding fast like hers. Fire pinpricked her skin as she surveyed that proud, angry face and felt his body's reaction. To *her.*

It felt glorious, *right* that they were in this together. This had nothing to do with duty. Seeing him grapple with the same desire evoked a pang of tenderness that only amplified her response to him.

Her legs were wobbly and there was a melting sensation low in her body. She shifted, realising the strip of silk and lace between her legs was wet with arousal.

'Nothing to say, Annalena?'

He spoke through clenched teeth, like a man struggling for control, which made her realise she should release her hold. But she didn't want to. For the first time in her life she wanted to take a step she'd avoided since she was old enough to understand desire could be dangerous. Instead of nerves she felt only anticipation, as if she'd waited for this moment. This man.

Rather than releasing him, she slid her hand lower, squeezing gently.

Colour streaked his high-cut cheekbones and his eyes glittered more gold than brown. His hips rocked forward in an explicit thrust.

'You want me.' The words tasted wonderful. 'I like that.'

A laugh cracked the taut air between them. His eyes blazed with approval but at the same time she saw his jaw clench, a muscle spasming.

Reluctantly she let him go, fingers twitching as she took a half-step back. Needing a second to absorb the enormity of the moment.

'And you want me.'

It was a statement not a question, and she nodded. They'd gone past prevarication and point scoring. Only honesty would do. 'Yes. I'm...curious.'

And awestruck. Excited and nervous. But above all she wanted more of Benedikt. Avoiding him wasn't possible. Abstinence made her a wreck. The need in her was too strong.

'We can work with curious.' He paused. 'If you agree.'

No sign now of that fierce amusement. His expression was grave.

'We're partners, Annalena. Husband and wife. We've committed our lives to our nation. Love isn't on the table. But there's respect and attraction. We're entitled to find what pleasure we can in a marriage neither of us sought.'

As he spoke he lifted his hand to trail his knuckles down her cheek. Annalena exhaled, turning into his touch, relieved as the barriers tumbled. This truth she could deal with. 'Yes. We're entitled to that.'

Because it was mutual passion, not one-sided yearning, which she couldn't have borne. She ignored the blip of her heartbeat when he'd acknowledged love was an impossibility.

'Respect and passion sound good to me.' She pressed her mouth to his knuckles, delighting in this connection between them.

'In that case…'

He drew her hard against him with one arm wrapped around her waist.

'I suppose you have no idea how you've tantalised me in this dress.' His gaze dropped to the narrow V of her neckline that plunged between her breasts. His stare shot fire into her blood and made her push her shoulders back. 'I thought brides were supposed to be demure.'

'I didn't want to look dowdy.' Especially when she'd feared some would expect that. 'My designer friend had this amazing design she said would be perfect, formal but feminine.'

Heavy ivory satin dropped in folds to the floor. Long sleeves fell in pleats that became soft, belling folds. A high collar plunged to a deep opening between her breasts and the whole bodice, which arrowed down to her abdomen in an almost mediaeval style, was heavily embroidered.

It was unlike anything she'd ever worn and she loved it. Wearing it made her feel feminine and powerful.

Especially when Benedikt looked at her like that, his gaze eating her up.

'She was right. It's perfect.'

His voice was gravel and had the same effect as flint striking stone. Sparks ignited across her skin. His hand dropped from her face to her collarbone and her breath stopped as skin met skin. Slowly his palm slid lower, the weight of it delicious. When he reached the place between her breasts he splayed his fingers.

'There's tape there,' she explained as he met resistance. But she needn't have worried. He found the double-sided tape that kept her breasts fully covered and deftly stripped it free.

Hadn't she said he knew his way around women?

Annalena sighed as her unfettered breasts eased towards the opening while Benedikt explored. Teased, more like. He stroked the inner curve of each breast, stretching his fingers under the fabric but not quite far enough to reach her pebbled nipples.

She grabbed his shoulders as arousal quaked through her.

'You like that, Annalena? What about this?'

He bent to kiss from her collarbone to her breasts. His tongue caressed the tender, sensitive skin bared to his caress, trailing ribbons of fire wherever he touched and making her hands clench into his shoulders.

She wanted him to touch her like that everywhere.

All too soon he stopped. Yet instead of rising to possess her mouth, Benedikt dropped to his knees. Pure gold gleamed in eyes that regarded her steadily while he grabbed the voluminous skirt, bunching it up her shins, to her knees, then higher.

Her breasts rose on a snatched breath as his smile became

QUEEN BY ROYAL COMMAND

a devilish grin. Breathless, she watched him skim his mouth over her inner thighs.

It was the most decadent thing she'd ever experienced. Even through sheer pantyhose, the touch of his mouth to her trembling thigh created a jolt of lightning, driving down through her body.

Her fingers curled into his shoulders as he pushed the heavy skirt up to her abdomen. Now his gaze wasn't on her face. From this angle his honed features looked taut, the pulse at his neck jumping as he surveyed what he'd bared.

'Push down your pantyhose, Annalena.'

It sounded like an order in that roughened voice and for once she didn't think to object. Excitement burred through her.

Wordlessly she hooked her thumbs through the waistband and slid the tights down.

'And the rest. I want you bare.' Though she wanted that too, hearing him spell it out made her pause for a millisecond. Instantly he looked up and what she saw in his face told her his brusque tone had more to do with his own excitement than the need to give orders. 'Please.'

She swallowed the knot clogging her throat and hooked her fingers into lace and silk, dragging pantyhose and underwear together down her thighs. But when she would have lifted one knee to free herself he stopped her. Not with words but the simple act of leaning in to brush his mouth across her thatch of blonde hair.

Annalena jumped and clung to his shoulders, her knees wobbling.

'You smell so good.'

The words vibrated against her skin, making her twitch and widen her stance, only to be stopped by the restriction of the tights above her knees. She should feel foolish standing, half undressed. Or embarrassed with Benedikt nuzzling her *there*.

She felt nothing of the kind. She liked it.

Cogent thought frayed when he adjusted his grip on her skirt so he could explore her folds with one hand while he kissed her.

Lips pressed as fingers stroked and her hips bucked. Annalena felt his smile but before she could react, his tongue followed the same route, pausing to swirl and press.

She gasped, a raw, keening sound that made the hairs on her nape stand up. Or perhaps that was because of where his fingers delved while his tongue worked that incredibly sensitive nub.

Her hands found his scalp, fingers in thick hair as if to stop him moving away. This was so amazing she didn't want it to end, even as her pelvis rolled against his touch, meeting his stroking.

She shuddered as delight bombarded her. Instinct, formed by a life governed by duty and work, told her anything that felt so impossibly wonderful had to be dangerous. Eyes she hadn't remembered closing fluttered open to discover Benedikt looking up at her.

She gasped, undone by the blast of emotion that hit her as she met that molten stare.

'Come for me, Annalena. Let go.'

How she wanted to. Yet some stubborn part of her resisted. It was only as he caressed her again and her hips rolled in response that she saw a flicker of movement in the corner of her eye.

Lifting her head, she caught a reflection in the antique mirror. A woman, mouth open and red-cheeked, hands clamped on the man kneeling before her, his head dark against bare skin and ivory satin.

Shock exploded as she saw him bend closer, his hand moving between her legs. She'd never seen anything, experienced anything so…

'Benedikt!'

Her cry went on and on, primal and triumphant as her body exploded in a climax unlike anything she'd known. Colours burst against closed eyelids. Showers of gold and silver rained down, molten. She felt the climax deep in her body as she rode his hand through the final, desperate throes of delight.

Ages later she was aware of her fingers tight in his hair and the hot, moist touch of his breath against her thigh. There were words too, murmured words she couldn't make out but which sounded like praise and gentling noises designed to soothe.

She didn't need soothing. Despite the rackety beat of her heart she felt lax as if every bone and muscle melted. Her legs gave way. 'Benedikt.' Her voice was unrecognisable. 'I need…'

He read her body quickly. An instant later he was on his feet, scooping her against his chest. His eyes glowed and his smiling mouth was wet with the taste of her. The sight of him made something roll over in her chest.

'I know. It's time to find a bed.'

CHAPTER TWELVE

DIVESTING HIS WIFE of her glorious wedding gown was an experience Benedikt would remember for years to come.

He felt alternately eager excitement and something else, strong yet tender, as he took in her hazy, slightly unfocused stare, her body blush and her fumbling efforts to assist. He felt a need to cherish and protect.

It was as if the orgasm he'd given her had truly undone her.

Sure! You don't think the long, long day and the stress of the past weeks have anything to do with it?

The proud, argumentative woman who didn't hesitate to question when she thought he was wrong, or step up to daunting royal responsibilities, lay limp and delectably biddable as he carefully wrangled her out of the dress that had driven him crazy since she'd walked down the aisle.

She'd looked...perfect, a word he rarely used.

He told himself it was because of the clever dress design. It harked back to ancient tradition with its embroidery, full sleeves and shape that drew attention to her small waist. Yet it was thoroughly modern with that tantalising slice of bare flesh that defied anyone to label it old-fashioned.

It's not the dress and you know it. It's Annalena. You

couldn't have chosen a better bride. She may be a novice at court but she understands duty and dedication to her people.

He wasn't thinking about duty or dedication as he dropped the heavy satin over the side of the bed.

His heart hammered as he surveyed her, bare flesh pink with the flush of satiation. She had a slender frame, gentle curves and long legs. Pale breasts tipped with rose pink. Pubic hair a dark, burnished gold. Her lazy green gaze made his blood rush and sizzle.

Slowly he stripped her fine pantyhose and the wet scrap of lace and silk from her legs, tossing them over his shoulder, watching her eyes widen then narrow, sending a bolt of fire through his belly.

Benedikt slowed his breathing, battling the urge to wrench open his trousers and plunge into her.

'Take down your hair,' he instructed, wincing at his tell-tale huskiness.

'Don't get too used to giving orders. And shouldn't you be undressing? Or would you like me to do that for you?' She propped herself up against the bank of plump pillows.

So much for his wife being undone by bliss. His wife! That would take some getting used to.

But he could definitely get used to having her in his bed. Especially when she surveyed him with a glittering challenge that held neither anger nor doubt but pure sexual anticipation.

Benedikt lifted his hand to his shirt, undoing the studs as Annalena shuffled higher in the bed, her breasts jiggling invitingly. He fumbled, fingers seemingly too big and clumsy, so he grabbed both sides of the shirt and tugged. That was better. Cool air caressed overheated flesh as he shrugged free.

The look on Annalena's face as she watched made him still for a second before reaching for his belt buckle. Her stare branded as surely as fire. That look—as if she'd never seen anything so good as his naked torso—ramped up the arousal he struggled to control.

She lifted her hands behind her head and her hair uncoiled, rolling down over one shoulder, past her breast, towards her waist. He swallowed over a scratchy lump in his throat.

Once more he was reminded of someone mediaeval. A maiden letting down her hair for a lover.

The eroticism of shining tresses against flushed feminine skin was new to him, a man experienced in the art of sex. Benedikt felt a beat of something harsh and unfamiliar, something dark and untamed. Sex had always been fun, a need, a release. Now he fought the idea it could be more.

Not because of her long hair. But because of the way each moment since he'd walked into her suite felt invested with deeper significance, a meaning he couldn't quite grasp.

Now who's letting weeks of stress affect them?

A frown wrinkled Annalena's brow, her attention going to his groin and his half-undone belt buckle. 'Why have you stopped?'

He smiled, taut facial muscles pulling. 'I'm taking a moment to admire you.'

To his surprise, the colour in her throat and cheeks intensified. She looked delighted, as if she weren't used to a lover's compliments.

No time to ponder that. Benedikt stepped off the bed, stripping away shoes, socks and the last of his clothes, retrieving the condoms he'd shoved in a pocket.

'You came prepared.'

He couldn't decipher her tone and forbore to admit he'd been carrying condoms for weeks. He knew she'd viewed him as an opponent but he hadn't been able to deny his rising hunger for her. Or the hope she'd admit to the attraction she'd been so determined to repudiate.

'I assumed you weren't ready to conceive a child.'

She sat higher, crossing her arms and inadvertently plumping up her breasts, making his shaft twitch as he rolled on protection. 'You assumed right.'

He nodded, trying to focus on the conversation, not the bewitching sight of tight nipples cresting her arms like treats displayed for him to taste. He failed. How could he not notice?

'Good. Nor am I.'

Though at some stage a child had to be on the agenda.

His mouth tightened. He was already doing what he could to secure the throne. So was Annalena. The thought of them coming together, solely to create an heir, felt wrong. Like the way his father had manipulated his mother, convincing her he cared for her to get the heir he needed. Not to mention access to her fortune and international connections.

'What is it, Benedikt? Having second thoughts?'

'Does it look like I am having second thoughts?' he asked as he turned to the bed, his erection heavy and his flesh too tight from the effort of holding back.

She shook her head but he saw the way her crossed arms tightened and the upward tilt of her jaw. He recalled how she'd believed him uninterested in her.

Did she still think, even a little, that he didn't desire her? He knelt on the end of the bed, knees wide, gripped her ankles and, in one quick movement, tugged till she lay flat before him.

'I want you, Annalena, and it has nothing to do with making an heir or satisfying duty.' Their eyes locked and he felt that familiar electric pulse between them. 'Frankly, I've had it up to my neck with duty. I refuse to take it to bed with me. This is personal. I want *you*. Just like you want *me*.'

He waited and eventually she relented, her eyes like emerald fire. 'I do. So much.'

Her words stroked fire through his already eager body but he made himself go slowly, kissing his leisurely way up from her ankles. The musky, enticing scent of female satisfaction teased as he reached silky inner thighs. But before he could settle between her legs and bring her back to the verge of climax, she wriggled and tugged at his shoulders.

'Not that. I want *you*.'

She'd get no argument from him. Making his movements slow, forcing himself not to rush, he moved higher, nudged her legs wide and settled between them. His eyes closed as a powerful throb of pleasure rocked him. Their bodies, naked together, evoked powerful magic. When he lowered his head to her breast and she wound her arms around him, pressing him close, need rose sharply.

His hand was between them, guiding himself to her slick passage when she spoke. 'I should tell you I haven't done this before. It mightn't be easy.'

Disbelief blasted Benedikt. And the desperate urge to ignore the words and bury himself deep.

He closed his eyes, lowering his forehead to her neck and exhaling slowly. It took a moment or ten, but finally he trusted himself to move. He lifted his head to discover her chewing the corner of her mouth. She looked earnest and adorable.

Adorable? The feisty woman who never conceded a point?

'I thought you should know,' she said quickly. 'In case it's difficult. It could be…not what you're used to.'

She was right. He'd never been with a virgin. Having seen the debacle of his parents' marriage, he'd shied from potentially emotional relationships. He'd only been with experienced women who understood he wasn't looking for for ever.

'It could be disappointing for you,' she murmured.

'I won't be disappointed, Annalena. But this may be difficult for *you*.'

The idea made his gut churn and a heavy ache settle in his chest. He'd do everything to ensure that wasn't the case but even so...

'That's okay. I know the first time mightn't be good. But hopefully the time after will be better.'

He rose to his knees, disturbed by her low expectations, even if he applauded her common sense.

Benedikt didn't want this to be anything less than wondrous for her. He should be pleased she was pragmatic but he wanted, he realised with startling clarity, to see stars in her eyes. He wanted her to come around him, muscles clenching and heart pounding, her cries of ecstasy filling the room.

He wanted Annalena to shatter with delight. Then turn to him again and again and again.

Nothing less would do.

Annalena surveyed Benedikt's serious expression and wondered if frankness had been a mistake.

She bit her lip and almost...almost wished herself elsewhere. But how could she wish to be anywhere but here, about to have sex with the one man who'd ever roused her to such passion?

'Why?' He frowned. 'Is there someone else? Someone you've been waiting for?'

The question flustered her. The head of his erection was notched at her core, the heat impossible to describe, yet he found time to interrogate her!

She shifted and was rewarded by the sight of muscles and

tendons in his neck and chest drawing tight. Relief pulsed through her at the visible proof he was strung out too.

'I was tempted but somehow it never seemed right.' She'd been raised to think of sex in terms of a committed, lifelong relationship. That and her intrinsic distrust of passionate love, courtesy of her parents' tragedy, had made her too ready to see flaws in the men who'd tried to persuade her into bed. 'Maybe my standards are too high.'

'Or you didn't meet the right man.'

Benedikt sounded smug, as well he might, looking like some immortal god full of devastating masculine power.

'You think you're the right man? You have to prove— Oh!'

He'd flexed his hips and she felt the strangest sensation as her body opened for him. There was weight and heat and a mix of trepidation and thrilling anticipation that tensed her whole body.

To her surprise, Benedikt didn't thrust further. He lowered his head to her breast, fondling and kissing, squeezing until she squirmed beneath him, inching her legs wider so his solid thighs sank between them.

There, that was better. With one hand he nudged her clitoris, stoking the fire, then pressed in, a little further this time. He was so big, so solid, she didn't know how this could possibly work, though of course it must.

She was bracing to take him when he withdrew, the heaviness of his shaft shockingly virile against her thigh as he lavished attention on her other breast. Meanwhile his fingers teased and stroked until everything gathered in a rush towards orgasm.

He stopped before she fell over the edge.

Blinking up, Annalena met his serious stare as he slid forward, prodding gently till her breath caught on the edge of being overwhelmed.

So it continued, Benedikt kissing and caressing, building up the need in her, letting her acclimatise to his possession, one slow centimetre at a time.

It was either the most thoughtful, considerate introduction to sex or a refined form of torture, designed to drive her out of her mind.

Her need was so intense, the suspense so great, that finally she lifted her knees and anchored them around his hips so he couldn't pull away. To make doubly sure she grabbed his buttocks, digging in her fingers.

'More,' she whispered. 'Give me everything.'

Above her his face was a mask of pared lines and brutal restraint. His nostrils flared. 'Everything?'

Heart thrumming, she nodded. He gathered himself and plunged deep, so deep there were no words to describe such intimacy.

Annalena blinked, trying to catch her breath.

Instantly Benedikt frowned. 'I hurt you?'

'No!' How could she explain? It felt too extraordinary. 'Not hurt.'

She hefted in air, feeling the friction of her breasts against his hairy chest. That distracted her, sending delight corkscrewing through her. Everything about him felt so good.

There'd been no pain. Trepidation, yes, and she realised her tension would have worked against her if not for Benedikt's patient attentions.

She felt his strain, saw it in his almost-grimace, and felt a wave of tenderness for this man who put her needs beyond his own. If she weren't careful, she might read too much into that.

'Show me more.'

The grimace became a surprisingly endearing lopsided smile. 'Demanding woman.'

She raised her eyebrows, delighted. 'I *am* a queen.'

'Ah. Well, then, if it's a royal command...'

Benedikt moved back then bucked his hips. Annalena clung tight through his rhythm of surge and retreat, slowly testing her own response. She thrilled at the sensations he evoked, gasping at each new level of heightened arousal, mutually shared.

His breaths shortened, his movements grew quicker and less fluid. He lowered his dark head, grazing his teeth at a tender spot on her neck she hadn't known existed. Fire jolted through her and when his fingers caressed her too...

White light exploded, engulfing her, drawing her up and up as she shattered into stardust. But still the ecstasy went on, so acute it had no beginning or end. There was only bliss and Benedikt, golden eyes, convulsing body and then hot, cushioning muscles drawing her close and holding her through the maelstrom.

Benedikt stood before the bathroom mirror, concentrating on the razor's glide through the shaving foam on his jaw. An electric razor wasn't good enough today, not when he'd seen the stubble burn he'd left on Annalena.

Hard to believe they'd only shared a bed for one night. It felt like more. It felt *momentous*.

So momentous, so different, it worried him. He couldn't recall anything like it. He shook his head and flicked excess foam from the blade into the sink.

Who was he kidding? It had been compelling, exciting, but not—as he'd imagined in the early hours—extraordinary. That had been his hormones talking. And lingering shock that his bride had been a virgin.

No wonder he'd felt that sudden surge of protectiveness.

Except, he realised, it couldn't have been protectiveness,

just surprise and the need to ensure she enjoyed the experience. Her pleasure added to his own and he wanted a wife who enjoyed intimacy, not who avoided it.

Protectiveness! The only protection she ever needed was from you. You've used her again and again, forcing her into marriage and a crown she doesn't want, just to safeguard your position. Making her give up a career she loves because you alone decided it was necessary. Revelling not only in her passion but her virginity.

He grimaced, avoiding his eyes in the mirror, not wanting to discover what he'd see there.

Today he'd woken to sunlight illuminating Annalena sprawled and exhausted in her rumpled bed. Because even her inexperience hadn't been enough to stop him having her again, and again, egged on by her enthusiastic responses.

Right. Blame her, when what drove you was your own selfish need. You might talk the talk but underneath are you any better than your father?

Benedikt winced as he nicked his throat, dark red blood welling against white foam.

That was what had catapulted him out of her bed. The fear that, despite the altruistic spin he put on his actions to protect the country, he was a chip off the old block. So intent on getting his own way that he saw others as necessary collateral damage.

Would Annalena really have been such a threat to the crown? He understood her well enough now to know she'd have abided by an agreement never to undermine his rule or that of his heirs.

Heirs.

His pulse quickened. Not because he was eager for kids, but imagining Annalena, rounded and ripe with his child. His visceral response was so profound he almost dropped the razor, finally collecting his wits and reaching for something to staunch the dribble of blood down his throat.

Despite the condoms it was possible he'd made her pregnant. They'd been very…enthusiastic and he'd enjoyed foreplay so much that at least once he'd been tardy putting on protection.

Yet he felt no panic, or sense of walls closing in as he had before when considering a family of his own.

Coming from a nightmare family situation, marriage and children had never appealed. Only the eventual need for a royal heir had made him consider taking a bride, hence his pragmatic interest in the Countess.

It wasn't just that his father had been cruel. Even without that, his mother would have been desperately unhappy, in love initially at least with a man incapable of softer emotion.

As for raising children… He'd always thought bringing a child into an unhappy family was a crime. He knew how a child could be used as both a hostage and a prize. Then there was the question of whether he had what it took to be a good parent. His father had been appalling and anything but a good role model and his mother, though she'd tried, hadn't been able to make up for her husband.

Listen to yourself! It's still all about you, isn't it? What about Annalena and her needs?

He rinsed the razor then washed his face, blotting it with a towel.

He couldn't give Annalena what she wanted. The full-time career to which she'd dedicated herself. A man who'd cherish her. She'd admitted when he'd first mentioned marriage that she'd hoped one day to find someone *right* for her. Benedikt knew that was code for love.

Pragmatic in other ways, she was still a romantic.

He didn't trust love. He'd never seen it work. It had brought his mother only unhappiness. Even his much-admired grand-father had married a woman who'd helped him make his first million.

But Benedikt would do everything to make this new royal life as easy as possible for Annalena. He'd respect and trust her.

They'd be partners. Partners with benefits.

He'd find a way to make that enough for her.

CHAPTER THIRTEEN

ANNALENA WOKE TO find her head turned towards the car window as they drove through darkness. Benedikt was beside her in the driver's seat. The vehicle was climate-controlled but she *felt* the warmth of his body and registered the unique tangy scent of his skin.

After last night's intimacies her physical awareness of him had turned into something more, as if he'd imprinted himself on her psyche and her body.

She knew she'd be able to *sense* his presence anywhere. She felt that awareness now in the pit of her stomach, a coiling consciousness, and in her chest, expanding as she inhaled that tantalising scent.

All the more reason to her keep eyes closed while she gathered her wits. It had been an eventful day and she needed to process it.

She'd woken feeling more alive than she ever had in her life. But disappointment had consumed her on discovering Benedikt's absence. They'd spent the night entwined, even when they weren't having sex. Annalena was careful not to confuse sex with making love. Even if that was what it had felt like—his gentleness, his care and his passion.

Just as well she was a pragmatist. She understood the way she'd felt last night, and her searing disappointment at his desertion this morning, must be products of her inexperience. Losing her virginity was a major event on top of weeks of strain and high emotion.

No wonder she'd felt so much.

When she became acclimatised to physical intimacy she'd be able to separate her emotions. It was just that last night had been so…

She had no words. Wonderful didn't encompass the depth of her emotions as she'd hugged Benedikt to her and felt him spill himself inside her. When he'd taken such care with her that it had seemed not like calculated patience but tenderness, almost reverence.

She stifled a snort. The illusion hadn't lasted. Waking alone and naked, the bed cold around her, had brought her back to reality.

They'd share the crown and their bodies but emotions weren't part of the deal.

Of course he'd had a plausible reason for leaving, as he'd explained over breakfast. He hadn't wanted to wake her, knowing she'd be exhausted and possibly sore. His solicitousness about that had made her blush despite her best efforts.

So, he'd explained, he'd worked in his own suite with the door open so he'd hear when she got up.

She *had* needed the sleep. And she wasn't sore but tender, aware of her body as never before. All day, at the most inconvenient times, she'd felt that tenderness, remembered last night and wished…

There's no point wishing for the impossible.

Despite Benedikt's solicitude over breakfast, there'd been no breath-stealing kisses, just reminders that theirs was a pragmatic marriage. He'd ushered her to a seat, his hand hovering close but not touching. As for a good morning kiss, he'd pressed his lips to her forehead as she'd sat and when she'd tilted her head up for more he'd already turned away to sit on the other side of the table.

They'd discussed allocating her a security detail and a private secretary. That was when he'd surprised her, asking if she'd like Udo, the guard she'd first met in the palace foyer, on her security team. She'd seen Udo several times in the palace and had always stopped to exchange greetings.

Annalena didn't know whether to be worried that such minor interactions had been noted, or pleased at Benedikt's thoughtfulness, suggesting a friendly face on the team she'd need, despite her protests.

When they'd discussed candidates for her secretary there'd been another surprise. 'As long as it's not Ida Becker,' Annalena had said.

Only to have Benedikt declare, 'Ms Becker has left palace employment.' Seeing her stare, he'd added, 'I discovered she was the one who rudely left you waiting that first day, and her attitude since...' He shook his head, his expression grim. 'I won't have her near you, or the palace.'

Benedikt's words, his protectiveness, had disarmed her. It was impossible to believe now that Ida had had a relationship with him. He had better taste and he wasn't the sort to dally with staff. When Annalena had accused him of toying with the Countess's feelings he'd looked appalled at the suggestion, and that was the woman he'd considered marrying.

Benedikt confused her. His thoughtfulness was real, as was his passion, but he deliberately distanced himself.

Organising a surprise honeymoon is hardly distancing himself.

That had been utterly unexpected. He hadn't mentioned a honeymoon, nor had she anticipated one, for they weren't ordinary newly-weds, eager to be alone together. The news that he'd organised one had stunned her. She knew his work-load. How had he carved out time for a bridal trip, and why?

Obvious. Benedikt wanted the world to believe theirs was more than a convenient marriage. He wanted it to appear solid.

Annalena remembered her shock as the motorcade had left the palace and headed, not for the airport, but towards Edelforst.

It seemed she was the only one who hadn't known. When they'd reached her province people had lined the roads in every town and village, sometimes even in forests and farm-land. Her throat had closed as she'd seen beaming faces, flags waving, and wildflowers strewn across the road. And when they'd taken the road to her grandmother's home...

'I know you're awake, Annalena. I can hear you thinking.'

Had his senses become attuned to her the way hers were to him? Then she realised how ludicrous that was. She sat up, blinking as the headlights cut the darkness, following a winding, well-made road.

'It was kind of you to visit my grandmother.' She blamed her scratchy voice on the fact she'd just woken. 'It meant a lot to her, and me.'

'She's a formidable lady. I can see where you get your strength.'

Annalena turned, surveying his profile in the light from the dashboard. Her heart did a funny little somersault and for a second she felt a jab of distress. Would it always be like this now? This weakness for a man who could never be the sort of husband she wanted?

'She's strong-willed, but she's caring too.'

Some people only saw Oma's formality and didn't re-alise the kindness that made her the special person she was.

A wry smile curved Benedikt's mouth. 'I know. It's there

in the respect her people have for her. And the obvious love she has for you. But I wouldn't like to get on her bad side.'

'I don't think you need worry about that. She approves of you.'

That hadn't entirely surprised Annalena, given Oma's comments about him as a potential husband. Yet she'd been surprised at how well the pair had got on. Oma had unbent enough to let him kiss her cheek, a rare privilege.

'I take that as a huge compliment. I admire her enormously.'

'I didn't think you knew her.'

'No, but I knew of her years ago. She was one of the few people in all Prinzenberg able to hold my father to account. I always admired the way she spoke up for what she believed was right, even when he tried to bully her.'

His words created an inner glow. 'She's been my heroine all my life.' And the closest she'd had to a mother.

'I thought she'd come to the capital for the wedding.' Benedikt glanced her way. 'You said she was unwell and so I didn't expect someone so spry.'

Annalena hesitated, about to prevaricate. But they'd agreed to be truthful with each other and there'd be other times when Oma's incapacity would become obvious.

'Not all disability is visible.' She turned to look at the windscreen, trying to work out where they were, but the forest wasn't familiar.

'Oma is strong in many ways but the trauma of my parents' death took a toll. She refused to enter the rest of Prinzenberg again, but when I was little I travelled with her regularly all through Edelforst. Then, gradually, I realised she wasn't travelling as far as before. Her physical boundaries have narrowed, even though her interests and her mind haven't. Nowadays she barely goes beyond our valley. People come to her instead.'

Warmth closed around her fisted hand. Warmth from Benedikt's long fingers, gently squeezing. 'Agoraphobia?'

Annalena nodded. 'I know she wanted to be at my wedding.' She'd wanted it too.

'I'm sorry she couldn't be. It was tough for you not having family there.' He lifted his hand to the wheel as they took a bend and Annalena was surprised how much she missed his touch. 'We'll just have to visit her often.'

Annalena's head swung around. In the dim light he looked serious, and he'd said *we* not *you*. 'You'd do that?'

'She's important to you and you to her. Why would I get in the way of that? My father was deplorable but other members of my family saved me from the worst of him. And from myself. If you have good people in your life you need to cherish them.'

That surprised her. Talk of cherishing seemed at odds with the tough negotiator who'd put their wishes behind the country's future. He seemed genuinely taken with her grandmother but to decide they should both visit her, as if he wanted to build a relationship with the old lady, was something she'd never considered.

Because you've spent so long thinking of him as your enemy. You know there's more to him than that.

Then there was his candour about his family. How had they saved him and from what? Did he mean his mother? But why not say so? Annalena was ashamed she had no idea what other family he had. None were at the wedding.

She was about to ask when Benedikt said, 'We're here.'

The car swung out of the forest, the road curving up to a wide-eaved chalet overlooking a meadow. Lights shone at the windows and along a deep balcony with a carved wooden balustrade where scarlet flowers spilled. High beyond the chalet sat the dark bulk of a mountain.

Annalena blinked. If Benedikt had said they were flying to New York or a private Caribbean island she wouldn't have been surprised. A private mountain chalet, for this was no bustling resort hotel, was the last place she'd have imagined him taking her.

That was reinforced when they neared the building and she saw part of the floodlit white stucco decorated with a large painting. Such paintings were a local tradition. This one represented the Almabtrieb, the autumn procession down the mountains as dairy herds, wearing bells and flowers, left their Alpine pastures for the valley. It was charming but a far cry from the glitz and elegant sophistication she'd thought he'd favour.

But how well do you know him?

Last night she'd begun to believe she knew Benedikt in ways no one else did. Nonsense, of course. He must have had lots of lovers. Hadn't she warned herself not to bring emotion into a purely physical connection?

'We can be private here. The security team will be in accommodation on the edge of the clearing.' He switched off the engine and she felt his eyes on her. 'You like it?'

Annalena turned. The chalet lights illuminated his strong, familiar features. But his expression wasn't familiar. He looked expectant and concerned, as if unsure of her reaction.

No. As if it *mattered* what she thought.

The thought snatched the air from her lungs. Was this an olive branch? Like visiting Oma straight after their wedding?

He looked like a man who wanted to please her.

'Annalena?'

She moistened her dry mouth and was unprepared for the shaft of searing fire that shot through her as his frowning eyes narrowed on the movement, lingering on her lips before lifting to meet hers.

'It's wonderful. In fact...'

'In fact?'

Did he lean closer? She swallowed, finding it hard to speak because she wanted to move closer and kiss him. Abruptly she sat back.

'It's the sort of place I'd have chosen.' Belatedly she tugged her gaze free and looked over the dark meadow, fringing forest and outline of craggy mountains. 'It's so peaceful.'

'I'm glad.' His hand captured hers and she felt that deep unfurling sensation, as if vital parts of her body softened and melted. 'I thought you'd had enough of cities and schedules for a while.'

Annalena's vocal cords tightened. Because, despite the jam-packed diary of appointments she'd seen him and Matthias pore over, Benedikt had conjured time away from the stress and busyness of royal life for her.

Because he knew she needed it. Even if he'd been partly motivated by public perception, she *knew* this trip wasn't part of his original plan.

'When did you organise this?'

Benedikt tilted his head as if surprised by the question. 'The beginning of the week. Why?'

She shrugged. 'I'm amazed Matthias managed to reschedule your diary so quickly.'

'It was a miracle. Anyone else would have quit on the spot when I raised it. I owe him a terrific bonus.'

She'd seen how hard Matthias worked. 'Good idea. Maybe a long holiday?'

'That's the plan, as soon as we train a couple of secretaries to stand in for him. Right now I'd be lost without him.'

'He didn't work for your father?'

It was a guess, but Annalena liked the man too much to believe he'd been part of the previous King's court.

Benedikt's deep chuckle was inviting and it struck her that here in the dim confines of the car it was far easier to talk than at the palace. 'Absolutely not. Matthias has been with me for years.'

Annalena had suspected as much. The pair had a camaraderie that spoke of mutual respect and friendship. Matthias was competent, friendly and honest. Interesting that such a man was so loyal to Benedikt over a long time. That told her a lot about her new husband.

'What are you frowning over, Annalena?'

'Just thinking what a formidable pair you are, turning things around for the better, taking on your father's administration and rooting out problems.'

Like removing Ida Becker, whose negativity and rudeness had no place in the palace. But there was far more. Annalena had heard enough in the past few weeks to realise wholesale changes were under way to how royal business was conducted and contracts let.

'You know, I think that's the nicest thing you've said to me. Thank you, Annalena.'

Benedikt's grin caught something in her chest, drawing it tight. To her astonishment, he lifted her hand and kissed it, lips lingering to brush slowly across her knuckles.

Suddenly it felt like last night all over again. The spark of desire and connection, the rippling sensation across her flesh and the softening low in her body.

Annalena's fingers tightened on his. 'You don't seem to mind touching me now.'

'Mind?' He frowned. 'I like touching you.' His voice dropped to a low note that made her tremble. 'You know that.'

'Do I? You haven't touched me all day.' Her chin lifted. 'Or kissed me properly.'

She'd instinctively avoided the subject but now the constraint between them had dropped.

'Ah.' He looked at their joined hands then to her. 'There were reasons.'

When he didn't continue she prompted, 'We agreed to be honest.'

Benedikt released her hand and leaned back against the door. Finally he spoke. 'I was...on unfamiliar ground.'

'*You* were on unfamiliar ground? I'd never had a morning after but you had.'

Slowly he nodded. 'That was part of it. I felt *concerned*. You'd been saving yourself for someone who clearly wasn't me. It brought home what I'd taken from you, the future you wanted and couldn't have... I regretted that.' He crossed his arms, all humour vanished. 'You *were* waiting, weren't you?'

Annalena tried to interpret his tone, stunned at the idea her inexperience had impacted anything other than his physical pleasure.

'No. Maybe.' She clasped her hands. 'I don't know. Oma would tell you I've always been career focused. I've been attracted to men but never enough to...' She shrugged, reminding herself she'd promised honesty too. 'I suppose I held back. For as long as I can remember romance and tragedy have been tangled together in my mind. I suppose that was a barrier.'

'Because of your parents.'

She nodded. 'I was never going to be swept off my feet. I'm too cautious for that. But I always imagined I'd find a partner and have children one day.' Benedikt looked as if he were about to say something but she'd had enough of this subject. 'You said there were reasons, plural, why you didn't touch me today. What was the other?'

Light danced in his eyes and the flat line of his mouth curved into a smile that made her pulse quicken. 'I was afraid if I touched you I wouldn't want to stop. And we had places to be, your grandmother to see.'

Her heart was doing a polka, or maybe following the rhythm of a sensual dance like a samba or tango. Because Benedikt wanted her, had wanted her all along. Her lips curved into an answering smile. 'Keeping your distance seems a bit extreme.'

'You think so?' His nostrils flared and his expression grew hungry. 'Do you have any idea how tough it's been, holding back? Making polite conversation with your grandmother and local dignitaries, meeting people in towns along the way. And all the time you've been beside me, close enough that I can smell your perfume and feel the warmth of your skin. But I haven't been able to take you in my arms.'

Annalena had told herself she wouldn't fall into those arms again, not easily. Because she'd yearned for his warmth from the moment she'd woken and he'd denied her that. As if what they'd shared last night was easily put aside.

Discovering his reasons broke down the wall she'd spent all day rebuilding.

Because you want him. You want the passion you discovered last night.

It was true, but she wanted more too. His tenderness and the sense of belonging she'd never expected but which had blown her away.

For a moment she felt that old caution rise. The fear of committing to something over which she had no control. But it was too late. She'd gone too far. She knew what she wanted and she wasn't going to deny herself because of some nebulous fear.

Anyway, what was the worst that could happen? They were committed to this marriage. It made sense to find what pleasure she could in it.

Annalena held his gaze as she unclipped her seat belt and reached for the door. 'Well, we've done our duty for the day. There's no reason to hold back any longer.'

Benedikt drew the cork from the bottle. The wine was pale gold like Annalena's hair as he poured it into an etched goblet.

With her bare feet curled beneath her on the sofa and a faint smile on her lips, she was entrancing. Every minute the housekeeper had spent giving them a tour of the place, Benedikt had chafed at the need for restraint.

He wanted Annalena. His need was tangible, a torsion in his body heavier and harder than anything he'd known.

Now the housekeeper was gone they were alone in the chalet. Yet he needed to maintain the veneer of a civilised man. He was mindful of Annalena's inexperience. She could be tender after last night. He turned away to pour the second glass.

'Benedikt.' Her voice came from just behind him. 'Put the wine down.'

He swung around, meeting sparkling green eyes less than an arm's length away. In the time it had taken to pour the glass she'd let her hair down. It rippled like a sunlit river over her shoulders and around her breasts.

He heard the chink of glass on silver as he put the bottle down, then he was drawing her close, an impossible mixture of relief and urgency sighing through his body as he pulled her flush against him.

Last night he'd told himself his celibacy over the last six months had made intimacy with Annalena seem unique. Or her virginity. Or his guilt. Even the fact it had been such a stressful time. Maybe they were all factors but here it was again, the sense that he'd found something both fragile and powerful. Something precious and new. Sexual desire on steroids but more too.

Dipping his head, he pulled her up and fused his mouth with hers.

Annalena wrapped her arms around his neck, grabbing his hair as she surged against him. He kissed her hard, delving between soft lips, one hand on her buttocks, pulling her to his pelvis. Fire streaked through him as she ground herself against his erection, making him buck hard.

Go slow. Go slow.

Reluctantly he lifted his head, dragging in air, lungs on fire.

Slumbrous eyes met his and something broke free inside. 'Benedikt, what is it?'

'I'm trying to pace myself. Not ravish you where you stand.' His facial muscles ached as he attempted a smile. 'I'm trying to be considerate.'

She lifted herself on tiptoe, in the process sliding up his aroused length and making him shudder. 'Can't you ravish me then pace yourself next time? I've waited so long.'

Annalena hadn't finished talking when he put both hands to her backside and hoisted her high. So good, so incredibly good. Especially when she wrapped her legs around his waist.

Benedikt stilled, poised on the brink of losing himself though they were fully clothed. No woman had ever affected him like this.

A minute later they were on the sofa, she sitting astride

him, arms around his neck, and they were kissing with a desperation that made him feel bizarrely as if he'd never done this before.

'Annalena,' he mumbled against her lips, stunned by how desperate he was. How much he needed her.

Her hands went to his belt buckle. 'Yes. Please.'

Benedikt must have found his wallet because soon he was sheathing himself, rolling the rubber on while Annalena watched. For a second he shut his eyes, needing to assert some self-control. Instead he felt soft fingers slide down his length.

Vice-like, he wrapped his hand around her wrist and pulled it away, shaking his head.

She pouted as if disappointed. Did she have any idea what that did to him? How often he'd fantasised about those plump lips on him?

Still holding her wrist, he burrowed his other hand under her skirt, grateful she'd worn it instead of jeans. Questing fingers met warm flesh then damp lace. One tug and it tore away. Over the thrum in his ears he heard Annalena's gasp but it was excitement, not outrage he saw in her shining eyes.

Releasing her hand, he pulled her skirt up. 'Come to me, sweetheart.'

He watched her shuffle closer, rising as she knelt above him.

'That's it,' he crooned, hands sliding around her hips. 'Now down.'

She paused as they came in contact, heat meeting heat, need against need. Then, with an ease that emptied his lungs of oxygen, she sank until they were completely joined.

Benedikt saw her wonder and knew she'd see the same in his eyes. It was utterly new to her but inexplicably it felt new to him too. He barely had time to register that when his primitive self took over.

His hands were tight on her hips as he thrust, pulling her to him. His mouth crushed hers. But as she rose then fell again, learning the rhythm, she slanted her mouth fiercely against his. Her fingers dug into his shoulders as the urgency he'd tried to rein in took them both.

It was a desperate, wild ride. Acute sensation, driving hunger and a crescendo of pleasure.

Benedikt felt pressure build at the base of his spine then in his groin. He couldn't last. He captured her face and poured all his jumbled yearning and unresolved emotions into their kiss, stunned to receive the same from her.

His hand slid to claim her breast and she jolted against him. He swallowed her cry, convinced he heard his name on her lips as they toppled over the edge together. His life force spilled into velvety heat as bliss took him.

CHAPTER FOURTEEN

ANNALENA SHADED HER EYES, squinting into sunshine. Her heart was in her mouth yet she felt a mix of awe and pride as she watched Benedikt climb the rockface.

The sheer rockface.

When she'd said as much he'd laughed and assured her there were plenty of hand and footholds on the cliff.

Nevertheless nerves nibbled her stomach. If anything happened to him…

A few short weeks ago she'd have thought it a solution to her problems to hear the new King had died. Now the thought made her shudder. Ten days after their wedding and so much had changed.

She'd changed and her feelings about Benedikt too.

With a final surge of flexing, impressive strength, he pulled himself over the cliff top. Then he stood, waving at her. He didn't even seem to be breathing heavily. Whereas her heart hammered and her breathing was shallow.

She waved back, smiling as he grinned. The breeze riffled his hair and he looked carefree and young, not the severe man she'd met in Prinzenberg.

She dropped her hand as he stepped out of sight to explore before walking down the steep but navigable slope beyond the rockface.

Annalena turned and sank onto the blanket where they'd lunched.

Each day they made love, hiked, and talked about everything and nothing. She told him about her fieldwork and her fascination with lichens and mosses. He talked of his time in the US and some of his climbing adventures.

She found herself ever more drawn to Benedikt. Even the word *husband* didn't faze her now.

It wasn't his looks. It was his essence, that charisma she'd always felt. His character. Far from being callous and unsympathetic, he was a man of compassion and deep humanity. A man who attracted her in ways that had nothing to do with sex.

Though the sex was phenomenal. Just thinking about their sex life made her toes curl.

Even his occasional retreat into thoughtful silence didn't seem negative now. Before, she'd imagined his every reaction a response to her, imagining him judging and finding her wanting. Now she saw a man who'd faced his own problems. Yes, he brooded occasionally but didn't she too sometimes? Usually she kept her own counsel, working through problems alone rather than turning to others. Once in a while she'd share concerns with Oma.

Who did Benedikt share with? Matthias?

To her delight he'd begun sharing with her.

He'd been open when they'd discussed his plans for the state, his reforms and snags blocking his way. Yesterday, picnicking by a mountain tarn, he'd mentioned problems in a local tender process and asked her opinion.

It had felt the most natural thing to thrash out the issues with him.

That was when she'd realised he already knew about her work, not only as a botanist. She'd done her share of contract negotiations. The centre where she'd worked, initially funded by an endowment from her grandparents, was at the forefront of research into Alpine plants. That research was leading to potential new medications.

Would she be able to continue her scientific work part-time? It seemed unlikely. She couldn't imagine life without it. She sighed. Was that the lot of all royals, putting their personal lives aside?

Annalena lay back on the rug and closed her eyes, wondering what dreams Benedikt might have set aside.

She was drowsing when a deep voice murmured, 'Sleeping beauty, I presume?'

Lips brushed hers, brushed and clung. She raised a hand to stroke Benedikt's lean cheek and thick hair. He smelt of mountain sunshine and tasted tantalisingly masculine. She sighed against his mouth as her body softened.

Would she ever get enough of him? Their sexual connection was amazing but it wasn't the whole of what she felt. Her link to him grew stronger with each hour yet she still had so much to learn about him.

Benedikt pulled back, expression unreadable with the sunlight behind his head. 'That was a big sigh. What were you thinking about?'

About how big my feelings are for you. About how I've begun to yearn for more.

Yearning was dangerous. He'd been clear in what he could offer—partnership based on duty with lovemaking to soften the edges. Because it *was* lovemaking, she realised, at least on her part. She mightn't actually be in love but she wasn't as heart whole as she'd once been. The realisation made her tremble.

'I was wondering about you, actually.'

'What exactly?'

She wished she could see his face clearly. 'What you'd do if you weren't King. What were your dreams? And,' she hurried on, 'you said your family saved you from your father and yourself—'

'And you want to understand.' His voice held an edge she couldn't decipher. Not anger but something hard. So she was surprised when he said, 'I know I owe you more. You've shared so much with me.'

Abruptly he moved away and Annalena was about to protest when she realised he was just leaning across to the picnic basket. 'Would you like to share an apple?'

She nodded, watching as he took a paring knife, neatly coring and segmenting the fruit.

He frowned as if in concentration, but his expression transformed into a teasing smile as he held a segment to her lips until she opened and took a bite, tasting crisp sweetness.

Satisfaction flared in those golden-brown eyes and, she'd swear, sensual interest. But for once Benedikt didn't pursue that. He put the knife away then leaned back, propped on one elbow, munching.

'What would I do if I weren't King? Easy. Focus on my business. I thought I had years left to pursue my own commercial interests.'

'Tell me about them.'

He offered her another bite of apple. 'I began in media and advertising. That's where my grandfather made his fortune. I still have some investments there in North America, but my main interest became IT. Software development, cyber security, a range of areas. I finance start-up companies. I suppose I'm drawn to the industry's creativeness. But I dabble in other things too.'

'You have a nose for business.'

He shrugged as if unwilling to accept praise. Most men she knew loved accolades but Benedikt wasn't most men.

'So, you'd devote yourself to business.'

That boyish grin returned and her heart pattered faster. 'I'd make time for mountaineering. And skiing.'

'I love skiing.'

'This winter, we'll go together.'

He leaned across and he offered her another piece of apple. She took a bite, watching him watch her, and felt a febrile thread of arousal run through her body. But she wouldn't let herself be distracted... Yet.

'I'd like that.' She imagined them speeding down the slopes, blood pumping from the exertion and exhilaration. Afterwards, alone in their chalet... 'But was business your dream when you were young?'

The shadow crossed his features. 'The only dream I had then was getting away from my father. You know what sort of man he was. He treated his family no better. He didn't care about anyone but himself.'

Benedikt paused, looking into the distance. What did he see? She was sure it wasn't the beauty of the Alpine scene.

'He destroyed my mother.'

The words were shocking for their matter-of-factness. Annalena had hoped he'd let her in, sharing details of his life, yet his frankness surprised.

'For reasons I never understood she cared about him. Their marriage was a convenient one but she loved him at least in the beginning. He took that love and twisted it into a weapon.'

Annalena sat up, covering Benedikt's hand with hers.

He gave her a tight smile. 'As for me, I was a necessary evil. He wanted an heir and insisted I do him proud yet he took every opportunity to alienate me. I think he resented the fact I'd eventually inherit. He didn't want to share power with anyone. Usually he'd ignore or belittle me, but other times he'd micromanage my life and he was never satisfied.'

'Oh, Benedikt! That's awful.' She'd been an orphan yet she'd known love and support.

'It's okay. *I'm* okay. I had my mother, when she was well enough, and I had her father, my grandfather. He was the role model who saved me.'

Benedikt squeezed her hand, darkened eyes snaring hers.

'You said your family saved you from yourself.'

After a moment he nodded. 'He and my mother. They showed me another way to live. Taught me to think of people other than myself.'

He huffed a laugh that didn't sound like amusement. 'My father insisted I spend my early years in the palace. Much as I learned to fear and loathe him, I also learned his ways. By the time he grew bored with being a father and let me travel to the States each summer, his poison had infected me. I was a sullen, selfish kid focused on myself, on getting what I wanted and, of course, keeping out of my father's way.'

His self-hatred astonished her and she leaned closer. 'You were only a child.'

Benedikt hitched those broad shoulders. 'A child raised by a cruel, narcissistic man. Being away from him, learning about kindness and decency, was like discovering a whole new world. I began to believe maybe I could find a place for myself in that world.

'My family had a lot of patience. They persevered through the bad behaviour, the acting out, the time in my late teens when I decided that despite everything I'd learned, selfish hedonism was the way to go.'

He looked down at her hand clutching his. 'With their

help I fought *not* to be like my father, even if sometimes I feel his darkness inside.'

Benedikt's words pierced her. 'You're not like him. How can you think it?' He raised a quizzical eyebrow but said nothing. 'You're dismantling everything bad he created in this country. You and Matthias.'

And now she was too. She felt an uprush of pride at the thought of helping that endeavour.

Finally he inclined his head, his mouth twisting as he lifted his hand to stroke her jaw. 'You're so earnest on my behalf. Thank you, sweetheart. After the way I corralled you into marriage that's kind of you.'

Annalena jerked her head back. 'Don't patronise me, Benedikt. It's not kind. I'm speaking the truth.'

That cynical twist of his lips disappeared and the bleakness left his eyes.

'That's something you always deliver.' This time his smile was genuine. 'After dealing with my father's Byzantine arrangements and secret back-room deals, it's refreshing to have someone who says what they mean and doesn't shy from the truth.'

'What else could you expect from a plain, unsophisticated scientist who spends more time with plants than people?'

'Plain? Unsophisticated? You're neither of those things.'

She hadn't been fishing for compliments. 'I meant—'

He leaned in, crowding her back towards the picnic blanket. 'You're anything but plain and you have one of the most sophisticated minds I know.' His eyes glinted with intent as her shoulder blades hit the ground. 'As for your looks, your body...' He settled over her, hard muscle against yielding flesh. 'You know I approve wholeheartedly.'

He nuzzled her neck, nibbling against that sensitive spot, making her gasp as need rose.

Annalena knew he was deliberately diverting her. She was amazed he'd shared such intimate details. Amazed and horrified that it wasn't just his father he viewed negatively, but himself.

Her heart felt raw. Remembering his stark expression as he spoke about darkness inside, she felt sympathy rise for the troubled boy he'd been and the man who devoted his life to others yet believed himself so flawed.

'Benedikt, you—'

His mouth covered hers in a caress so potent it thickened the blood in her veins and the thoughts in her brain. She cupped his face in her hands, holding him to her as she opened for him, curling her tongue against his lips and inviting him in.

He accepted the invitation. His mouth was hard and needy, his hands too, though she felt the restraint he tried to impose on himself.

The air turned smoky with searing need, the sharp tang of arousal in her nostrils, the taste of desire and Benedikt in her mouth.

He was iron hard against her belly as he lifted his head enough to meet her eyes, his blazing like molten metal. She felt him tremble, this powerful man who was so much stronger and better than he believed. 'I need you—'

Her fingers on his lips stopped his words, her heart curvetting against her ribs as she read his desperation. Her need quickened. 'Then take me. I want this. I want *you*.'

She shuffled her legs wider, glad that she'd worn a skirt in today's heat. Anticipation spiked as he settled lower. Minutes later she was naked from the waist down and his trousers were around his thighs, his erection sheathed.

She saw the tendons in his throat jerk as he swallowed. He nudged her entrance. 'I can't do finesse. I—'

'Shh…'

She wrapped her arms around his neck, drawing his mouth to hers as she lifted her knees to cradle him. Benedikt drove home, slow and deep, impossibly deep. Nothing had ever felt so good.

A sigh wafted on the still air, followed by a deep groan as all the energy he'd leashed erupted. He bucked, his movements jerky and her attempts to match his rhythm more clumsy still. But within seconds she felt that telltale quiver, the spasm of muscles, the unstoppable force.

Annalena clutched him close, her hand on his skull holding his face to her neck. Hot breaths on her throat, his possessive hand at her breast squeezing with just the right pressure. And between her legs and deep inside, Benedikt, stealing her soul and flinging her into rapture.

He shouted, her name thrown up to the sky, his throat arching as he pounded into her and she met him with mindless abandon. Finally they collapsed, spent, and a wave of tenderness swept through her as she held him tight.

Much later, when she opened her eyes and looked into the blue sky above, the world looked different.

Benedikt pulled Annalena into a deserted anteroom, pushing the door shut and drawing her close. She came eagerly, eyes shining, smile alluring. She wore red lipstick to match the dress she'd worn to the lunch they'd hosted for charity volunteers. All through the proceedings he'd wanted to haul her to him and kiss the scarlet lipstick away.

His wife was tempting, gorgeous, sexy and clever. She was overcoming her hesitancy about taking on a royal role and he couldn't imagine doing his job without her. She had a way of connecting with people that he wished he'd learnt.

He was improving but he doubted he'd ever have the knack for it that she did.

The day she'd stormed into his office and made her ultimatum was one of the best of his life.

She made him feel… She made him *feel*.

In the past he'd avoided emotion and what he had felt had often been negative, a trait inherited from his father.

Warm fingers stroked his cheek. 'Why the serious face, Benno?'

Even after four months of marriage, his heart thudded when she used the diminutive so tenderly.

His mother had loved him but was often unwell, retreating to her rooms. His grandfather had shown his affection, but never through soft words. His wife, with her directness tempered with warmth, was a revelation.

His Lena. Did she have any idea how she'd changed his world?

'I'm calculating if there's time to ravish my wife before my meeting.'

Her gurgle of laughter flowed like warm honey through his veins. 'You know there's not. And I promised the research team I'd review the draft report this afternoon.'

He nodded, pleased they'd found a way to give her a couple of days each week to pursue the vocation she loved. His arms tightened, pulling her flush against him, torture for both of them, but impossible to resist.

Mischief sparked in her eyes as she pressed her hand to his burgeoning erection. Sheet lightning blasted his vision as she tugged his belt.

'But we do have a little time.' Her smile turned sultry as she sank to her knees. 'I could—'

'No!' He pulled her high against him and the impact of

soft femininity against urgent arousal almost undid him. He clenched his teeth. 'What I need is *you. All* of you.' He watched her turn rose pink, lips parting. 'Besides, I'd never be able to concentrate on the meeting. I'd be in a stupor of sexual satisfaction.'

She slid her hand over his lapel, pouting. 'So what do you suggest?'

'I'm sure I can finish early. In the meantime we'll have to be satisfied with a kiss.'

'Not what I want to hear, Your Majesty, but I suppose it will have to do.'

'Believe me, Your Majesty,' he murmured against her throat, feeling her shiver, 'it will be worth waiting for.'

Inevitably he was late for his meeting, but Lena had insisted on combing his tousled hair and removing the lipstick smudges. Fortunately Matthias and his new team had used the time to brief the attendees, so in the end the meeting finished in good time.

Benedikt should dally with his wife during business hours more often. Now he'd put the time to good use, getting through some of his mail.

But his thoughts were of her as he settled at his desk.

They worked well together. She lightened his darkness and called him on his autocratic tendencies. Matthias tried but had to concede if Benedikt pushed the point. Lena conceded nothing.

He opened his emails, a flagged message catching his attention.

Urgent. Confidential. Legitimacy of Sovereignty.

Benedikt's heart missed a beat then quickened as he

opened it. He read the missive quickly then again, testing every word, ensuring he didn't miss any detail.

Finally he sat back, heart pounding and adrenaline thundering. This changed everything.

CHAPTER FIFTEEN

ANNALENA HURRIED DOWN the corridor. Her old laptop had died and though IT had promised to fix it quickly, she'd belatedly realised there was an urgent item she'd promised to read.

She *could* have made do with her phone but instead made for her husband's office.

Any excuse to see him!

Once that would have disturbed her, now it made her smile. Where once there'd been distrust, now there was intimacy, emotional intimacy. Trust and, with it, hope.

Hope that their convenient, dynastic marriage had become something more meaningful.

She hugged that hope to herself as she turned a corner. Benno respected and cherished her. He might not realise it but he'd changed, as she had.

How much she'd changed! She remembered opening her eyes and seeing the world altered. Because she'd finally made sense of her feelings. Benno was complex, with faults and strengths. He wasn't always right and he still tended to think his way was the best way, but he listened and he genuinely cared.

He understood how she thought and, so often, how she felt. They'd both been trained to keep emotions hidden and sublimate their own wishes for the greater good. With Benedikt she felt truly *seen* for the first time.

He could be so tender, so generous. So lovable.

She was in love with her husband!

Instead of her thinking that a disaster, it gave her hope for the future.

Look at the trouble he was going to, converting a more modern part of the palace into their private accommodation. Far from the state rooms, it would be comfortable and streamlined, with no overblown ornamentation, and it would have an unrivalled view of the pretty walled garden. He knew how much she loved that.

With a rap on the door and a smile on her lips, she entered, only to discover the offices empty. Matthias and Benno were absent.

Huffing a sigh of disappointment she made for Benno's desk. He wouldn't mind her logging on to access her mail.

He mustn't have gone far for the screen was still on. She settled in the chair, about to minimise that screen when something caught her eye.

Urgent. Confidential. Legitimacy of Sovereignty.

She didn't consciously decide to open it but a second later she was reading the extraordinary message sent by a legal expert who'd unearthed a long-forgotten document.

To rule in their own right, future sovereigns must be the child of a member of the House of Prinzenberg and born into a marriage that was celebrated publicly in the Royal Cathedral of Prinzenberg.

Annalena stared, unable to believe what she read. There was more, extolling the importance of giving the public certainty about claimants to the throne.

The lawyer explained there was no doubt the document was real and valid. He'd confidentially checked with the most senior constitutional lawmakers. So, he concluded, he felt it necessary to bring this to His Majesty's attention, given the current unique situation.

He means you sharing the crown with Benno.

Benno must have consulted the man about his options when she first came to the palace.

She swallowed. Benedikt's parents had married in the cathedral but hers hadn't.

This document destroyed her claim to the throne.

Oma had always said her parents had planned to renew their marriage vows in public, at the cathedral. Was this why? Had they known about this decree? Whatever they'd intended, it hadn't happened because her father had died.

So you never had a claim to the throne.

Oma couldn't have known that.

Benno's power-sharing deal, his marriage offer, was based on a lie. Her threat to take the crown from him had been no threat at all.

She pressed a hand to her throat where it felt as if her heart were trying to escape. The whole basis of their marriage was invalid.

Aghast, she looked at the date of the email. Two weeks ago. She slumped back in his chair, disbelieving.

He'd known for a fortnight and hadn't said a word to her! Why? Annalena's nape prickled, skin tightening as a chill enveloped her.

So much for trust, for sharing.

She pressed her other hand to her churning stomach. While she'd been reading so much into their improved relationship, Benedikt had kept this from her.

She'd believed their relationship was open and honest. *Special*. Yet he'd lied by omission.

Lied about something fundamental. For two weeks!

Did Benno, the man who'd inveigled his way into her trust and her heart, truly exist? Or had she imagined him, reading too much into physical intimacy and her husband's efforts to make their relationship easier? Had he simply been making the best of it? He'd said more than once that sex was their compensation for a dynastic union.

Said too that love was off the table, and after his revelations she understood that love wouldn't come easily to him. His dysfunctional family had damaged his view of himself and his ability to trust.

Had she let great sex and a little consideration turn her head? Had she confused physical intimacy with real affection? It didn't seem possible, yet...

She shot to her feet and crossed the room, as far from the email as she could get. Backed up against a bookcase, she wrapped her arms around her middle, fighting shudders as she thought back over the past two weeks.

He'd been more distracted though he'd denied it. Meanwhile he'd encouraged her to devote more time to her scientific work. Her heart had melted when he'd called that work valuable, saying it would be criminal for her to give up her career completely. When he'd suggested a plan to give her more time for that, devoting only a few days a week to royal obligations, she'd rejoiced.

You thought he cared. But maybe it wasn't that at all. Maybe it's the first step in...

Separation? Divorce? Unseating her from the throne?

Once she'd have jumped at anything that took her away from royal responsibilities. Now she'd begun to feel pride and satisfaction in some of them, feeling she was contributing to her country. The work stretched her and she welcomed that.

But her husband didn't need her any more. He encouraged her to spend more time at the research and development centre in Edelforst. It had been *she* who'd hesitated. Because she didn't want to be away from him, restricting herself to working from the palace except when they visited Edelforst and she'd catch up with her colleagues and Oma.

While you were dreaming of happy-ever-afters and a family with him, he was pushing you away.

Could it be true? Everything rebelled at the idea.

You're the wife he had to have. Never the wife he wanted. Now he's learned he doesn't need you and he's already looking for distance.

Had she been living a fool's dream, building castles in the air? She *knew* he didn't love her. Just because she'd fallen in love with him, she'd told herself he might eventually feel the same way about her.

The fact is, he's happier without you around. You were always the outsider. You never fitted here. You weren't even his first choice of bride!

Her emotions hit rock bottom. Did he feel *anything* for her apart from lust? As for manipulating her towards a separation via the career she loved, did he think that the easiest way, or was he trying to be kind?

The thought he might *pity* her, on top of his deviousness, was the final straw.

She dragged in a shallow breath then another and another but couldn't suck in enough oxygen. She needed to think and she couldn't do that here.

Swallowing choking emotion, furious with herself for her naivety, Annalena stumbled from the room.

* * *

Benedikt's worry grew when he found their new rooms deserted, bar the team refurbishing the floorboards. He'd pinned his hopes on finding her there. He'd already tried their current suite and questioned every staff member he saw, but none had seen Lena.

Returning to the office twenty minutes ago, he'd only got as far as Matthias's desk when his assistant said he'd seen the Queen hurrying down the corridor, visibly upset.

Matthias never exaggerated and Lena never broadcast her emotions in public. If she looked upset something was badly wrong. Benedikt had spun on his heel and gone to find her.

Unease gripped him. What had happened? Why hadn't she waited to talk with him? He'd thought they could discuss anything now that she trusted him.

Lena spoke with him openly and they'd found commonality in their odd childhoods, separate from their peers, always different, coping with others' expectations while finding their own way in the world.

He'd told her things he'd hugged to himself all his life. Lena insisted that his tendency to strategise and command weren't proof that he'd inherited even worse traits from his father. She saw positives in his character and her habit of asking for clarification on decisions made him pause more often now before taking action.

She'd changed his life, given him so much.

The thought of her hurting created a physical ache.

His gaze lighted on the walled garden beyond the window where his mother had so often sought refuge. Had Lena gone there too? He strode towards an exit.

Pausing outside the summerhouse, he breathed deep. Whatever was wrong, Lena needed him strong and supportive.

'Lena! Sweetheart?'

For a moment he didn't see her against the light streaming in the windows, then a shadow shifted, a figure moving to sit up straight on the sofa.

Relief caught his breath as he strode across and sank down beside her. 'What's wrong?'

Her mouth was drawn with pain and her eyes were pink and puffy. His alarm intensified. Lena didn't cry. Even when he'd cornered her into an unwanted marriage she'd been upset and defiant, not teary.

'Your grandmother?'

Had something happened to the old lady? The two were close. He reached for Lena's hand but she pulled away.

The gesture, small but definite, made everything inside him go cold and still. 'Lena, what is it?'

Instead of turning to him as he'd got used to, she fixed her gaze on the far side of the room. Something surged inside him, a stark emotion so powerful he'd swear his heart stopped.

'I needed time alone to think.'

Her voice was dull, her shoulders slumped. This wasn't the woman he knew. And why time alone? Often as not they shared the challenges facing them, bouncing ideas off each other. Just yesterday Lena had used him as a sounding board for a complication that had arisen in her research team.

'Talk to me, Lena. What's on your mind?'

Slowly she turned, chin lifting in that familiar way. But there was something different this time.

'It's been good getting back into more research work. I missed it and you're right, it's really where I belong.'

He frowned, not liking the finality of her words or the implication he thought that was the only place she belonged.

'You don't need me here and I'm much happier in Edelforst.' She moistened her bottom lip. 'I want to live there full-time.'

'What?' It was so unexpected Benedikt had trouble believing his ears. 'You mean until you finish this current project?'

Her gaze slipped away. 'I mean permanently, at least in time.' Deep green eyes met his and the force of her tightly leashed emotion rocked him back in his seat. 'After the first few years, your mother lived most of the time in the US. The country will survive if I move back to Edelforst.'

Benedikt felt his jaw sag, his mouth drop open. It wasn't only what she said, it was the way she said it, the way she refused to let him in. He *felt* her roiling emotions but she blocked him like a stranger.

He wanted to remind her they were married. That their relationship grew stronger and better every day. They were joint rulers of a country that needed them. Her words were a hammer blow to the chest. He could barely catch his breath.

'Why, Lena? Tell me the truth. We've been happy together.'

Something shimmered in her eyes and hope stirred. But then she shook her head. 'I thought I could do this, but I was wrong. I don't want a dynastic marriage for the country's sake. I want a *real* marriage, not a power-sharing agreement. I want to be with a man I can *trust*, someone I can believe in.'

Benedikt felt his blood freeze. 'You don't trust me?'

Her long pause carved a chasm through his soul. The fact she hurt him so easily should have surprised him, for he didn't *do* emotional relationships. But deep down he'd known Lena was different. *They* were different.

Their marriage wasn't like any previous relationship, and that had nothing to do with duty or public expectations. It had everything to do with Lena and how she made him feel.

Yet now she swept all that aside, everything he'd felt and hoped, as if they meant nothing.

'You don't believe in me? In us?'

The words almost choked him. For the first time in his life he'd let down his guard. Being with Lena had made him want to believe in a better life, in *them*.

'How can I when you lie to me?'

His head jerked back as if she'd hit him. Didn't she know him better than that? It was one more lacerating hurt. Each felt deeper and more devastating. Had nothing about their relationship been as it seemed?

How could he have been so wrong about her feelings? He knew he had little aptitude for deep relationships but he'd been so sure...

'We promised each other honesty and I've never lied to you.' His voice ground low as he forced out the words. 'I'm not my father, Lena. How many times do I have to prove it?'

Finally hurt gave way to anger. Bruised pride surfaced, but it was no consolation for the anguish that twisted him inside out.

For the first time he'd opened himself fully to another person. He'd ignored the tough lessons that had taught self-reliance and a mistrust of emotion. He'd trusted and felt and believed in things he never had before.

'You're lying now, Benedikt.' Her voice a curious mix of ice and heat as she spat out his name. 'For two weeks you've known I had no claim to the throne and what did you do? Instead of telling me, you pushed me away, saying I should spend more time away from the palace. What was the plan? To gradually edge me out? Isolate me then divorce me? Well, don't bother. I'll divorce you and renounce my claim to the throne.'

Lena surged to her feet only to halt, swaying as if unsteady. Benedikt was at her side in a moment, grasping her arm and turning her to face him.

Despite her fiery words her face told another story and it broke his heart. Her chin crumpled, her mouth quivered as she blinked. 'Let me go. I want to be alone.'

'I don't believe you.'

He loosened his grip so she could step away if she wanted. She didn't move and hope leapt.

'You're right. I should have told you about that email immediately. I tried to bury it, hoping it would go away.'

'Go away?' Her glittering green gaze, sharp as a faceted emerald, snared his. 'Don't you mean hide it until the time was right to push me away fully?' Her face pinched. 'It doesn't matter. I know the truth and that you want—'

'You don't know what I want!'

He tugged her to him, bodies colliding, and felt some of his impossible tension ease. This was where he needed her. He wrapped his arms around her, feeling a hit of satisfaction when she didn't pull free.

'I was never going to push you away, Lena. I don't want you going anywhere.'

His heart curled over on itself as she angled her chin up in a gesture of defiance, belied by the misery on her face. Her gallantry, her fighting spirit as she tried to hide hurt, made everything he felt for her well up.

'You expect me to believe that, when you hid something *so* vital from me? I was idiot enough to believe we trusted each other but I was wrong.'

He stroked his hands up her arms. 'I didn't tell you about the email because I wanted to protect you. I double-checked and that clause doesn't delegitimise your position as joint ruler.'

'But it means I could never have ruled alone. I was never

a danger to your authority. The whole basis of this farcical marriage no longer exists.'

Benedikt winced. She couldn't really think their marriage farcical. His heart thudded faster. 'I don't care about that, Lena.'

'You say that, yet you've done everything you could to encourage me back to scientific work.'

'Because I thought that made you happy!' He paused when he heard his voice grow strident. He leaned closer. 'I want you happy in this marriage. I want you to feel fulfilled. I know how much botany means to you. I was afraid you'd grow to resent a life spent focused only on regal obligations.'

Her eyes widened, doubt glimmering.

'It doesn't matter now what some fusty old document says. We're married and I want us to stay that way.' He dragged in a deep breath, chest rising against hers as he struggled to find words for what he felt. 'What we've shared has changed everything. It's changed *me*.'

'You don't want to rule alone?'

Her hands had crept to his upper arms. Was that a good sign or did she just need support?

'No, I don't, but this isn't about the crown—'

'It's all about the crown. It always has been.'

'Not any more.' Benedikt gathered her closer, fitting her snug against him. 'This is about *us*. I said I'd changed and I meant it. What I feel for you, Lena, it's taken over everything. It's bigger than duty or Prinzenberg. Nothing is more important to me than your happiness.' To his amazement his voice wobbled. 'You make me feel things I've never felt before. You give me perspective and happiness. For the first time I feel like my life, *our* life, could be about joy and fulfilment, not just obligation and work. I want to make you happy.'

Gentle hands cupped his face, wondering eyes holding his. 'Why didn't you say anything if you felt that way?'

'You doubt me?' His shoulders lifted. 'I shouldn't be surprised. I doubted myself. I told you about my upbringing. I've always had trouble trusting, much less forming meaningful relationships. I told you love wasn't on the agenda.'

'Love!'

'Yes, love.' He drew a sustaining breath but found he didn't need it. The truth wasn't such a challenge after all. 'I love you, Lena. I want to spend my life with you and that's got nothing to do with the crown. I should have told you about the email but I was afraid you'd fret about being here under false pretences or...'

'Or what?' He couldn't read her expression.

'Use it as an excuse to leave me.'

He hadn't admitted that even to himself before this moment. It made him realise that once again he'd manipulated things to get what he wanted, hiding what Lena deserved to know. He'd talked about trusting her but he'd still tried to take control for his own selfish ends. Horrified, he dropped his arms and stepped back.

But Lena followed, closing the gap so they were toe to toe. '*That's* what you thought?'

He swallowed. 'I didn't know.' Had he blown his chance of happiness, proving himself unable to relinquish control and trust her? The thought sickened him. 'I thought you were happy, I hoped so. That means everything to me.' He shook his head. 'But you're right. I owed you the truth. I convinced myself that document didn't matter because it didn't affect what we have now. It was a convenient lie because I wasn't sure you felt the same way about me.'

'Hiding an explosive secret like that,' she murmured. 'That's extreme. I would have found out some time.'

'I wasn't thinking clearly.'

'I know the feeling.' To his amazement she placed her palm on his chest. He felt it like a brand, the way she'd branded his heart as hers. 'I know the feeling exactly.' Her voice dropped. 'That's why I was so upset, because I'm in love with you, Benno, and I thought you wanted to get rid of me. I decided to pre-empt you and go straight away.'

His heart gave a mighty jolt as she called him Benno. As if he really was forgiven. He covered her hand with both of his. 'You love me?' The sick feeling in the pit of his belly disappeared, replaced by warmth. 'How can you after what I did? I should have been honest with you.'

'You're not the only one. We should have talked more about our feelings, but I was too scared.' A soft smile trembled on her lips. 'Do you really—?'

'I really love you.' Just saying the words made him feel ten feet tall. 'I never believed I could feel anything as glorious as this. I was an idiot and I was scared. I could say I thought it was too soon to tell you how I felt but it was fear that held me back.'

She nodded and lifted his hands to her mouth, pressing kisses across his knuckles, making his heart melt as his fingers curled around hers. 'I was the same. I never expected to feel this way.'

Benedikt drew in a shaky breath. He felt as if he'd swallowed the sun, as if she'd given him the moon and the stars. But all he wanted was her, his precious Lena.

His voice was as serious as when he'd made his vows in the cathedral. 'I promise to be completely honest with you, my love, including about my feelings.'

'And I promise to be completely honest with you, my darling husband, *especially* about my feelings.'

For a moment they stood solemn and still, eyes locked on each other. Then Benedikt drew her towards the sofa.

'In the interests of complete honesty,' he murmured, 'I need to be upfront about my intentions.'

'Intentions?' The glimmer in her eyes made his breath hitch. 'Tell me more.'

Benedikt sat down and pulled her onto his lap. As she settled, warm and soft in his embrace, eyes turned to his, he knew this was going to be all right. More than all right, it was going to be perfect.

'We did this the wrong way around. We married but had no courtship. I intend to rectify that, starting now.'

'You're going to court me? I like the sound of that.'

He nuzzled the base of her neck, drawing in the scent of flowers and Lena. 'Good. I need to do this thoroughly. It could take months.'

Her chuckle was liquid sunshine as she put his hand to her breast. 'Definitely, my darling. Maybe even years.'

Her darling.

His heart had never felt so full. And this was only the first day of the rest of their lives together.

EPILOGUE

THE CASTLE OF EDELFORST had never looked so good. Chandeliers glittered, mirrors shone and flowers scented the air as guests mingled in the ballroom.

From the minstrels' gallery above, music began and the guests retreated to the sides of the room. Annalena watched a couple approach and her breath caught. Even now her husband had that effect, especially when he wore formal evening dress.

They'd been married a year today. A year that had been blissful and challenging. They were both strong-willed and didn't always see eye to eye, but the promise of honesty had seen them through both testing and wonderful times.

In his stark clothes Benno looked incredibly sexy but serious, as befitted a king. But then, uncaring of the crowd, he lifted his hand and blew her a kiss, stealing her heart all over again. There was a ripple among the throng as women sighed in delight.

The man Annalena had met a year ago was still there, conscientious and determined. But now Benno embraced happiness with an enthusiasm that transformed him.

She smiled as he escorted her Oma, resplendent in navy and silver, onto the dance floor. Annalena turned to the man beside her. Young and handsome, Harald Ditmar said, 'Ready, Your Majesty?'

She nodded first at Harald then at his beaming grandfather, the colonel, who sat with his ankle strapped up. 'Absolutely.'

The crowd applauded as the musicians struck up a waltz. Annalena circled the room with Harald, while Benno and Oma danced in the opposite direction.

Incredible to think it was only a year ago that she'd attended her first royal ball. Now, confident in her abilities and in Benno's affections, she no longer felt like a fish out of water. She actually enjoyed dressing up once in a while, though she'd remove the emerald and diamond tiara after the dancing.

When the waltz ended the couples met. Oma's cheeks were flushed and her eyes glittered as she thanked Benno for the dance. 'But one waltz is enough for me.' She turned to Harald. 'Let's go and check on your grandfather, young man.'

'She really is a wonderful lady,' Benno murmured as the pair left and he gathered Annalena close.

'She's absolutely delighted we're celebrating our anniversary here.' His smile warmed her as the music began and other couples spilled onto the floor. 'Thank you for suggesting it.'

He shrugged as they began dancing. 'It's good to celebrate with family. Besides, we can head up to the chalet tomorrow for a break.'

He'd bought the chalet where they'd honeymooned as a belated wedding gift. Weekends there were some of their happiest times.

As they moved down the room Annalena frowned. 'They're playing the same music again, that's unusual.'

'I asked them to. Do you like it?'

It was light and lovely. 'I do. I've never heard it before.'

Golden brown eyes met hers. 'You wouldn't have. It's "Lena's Waltz". I commissioned it for you. Happy anniversary, my love.'

Annalena's eyes widened and she would have stumbled but for Benno's encircling arm. 'You commissioned a waltz?' What an amazing gift, especially from a man who'd once been totally absorbed in business and strategy, with no time for anything that wasn't 'useful'. But her husband was caring and thoughtful and knew how she enjoyed music. 'Oh, Benno. That's...' She swallowed.

He tsked in mock admonishment but smiled tenderly as he swung them into a turn. 'No need to get emotional.' He pressed a kiss to her forehead. 'But I love that you like it so much.'

'Like it? It's so special.'

'*You're* special.'

There she was blinking again but how could she help it when he looked at her like that? On the other hand she did have another reason for feeling a little emotional. 'You'll have to wait until we're at the chalet for your gift.'

How would he react to the news she'd had confirmed this morning, that they were going to be parents?

She didn't have to wonder. She knew he'd be thrilled, and he'd make the best father.

His breath tickled as he murmured, 'You're plotting something, Lena. Perhaps I'll have to persuade you to tell me about it when we're alone tonight.'

She grinned in anticipation, thinking of Benno's persuasiveness. Besides, they'd promised not to keep secrets and this was one she couldn't wait to share.

'That sounds like a wonderful idea, Your Majesty.'

* * * * *

If you couldn't get enough of
Queen by Royal Command
then make sure to catch up on
these other emotional reads
from Annie West!

His Last-Minute Desert Queen
A Pregnancy Bombshell to Bind Them
Signed, Sealed, Married
Unknown Royal Baby
Ring for an Heir

Available now!